Free to Love
(A prequel to *On Cue*)

Bettie Boswell

M Zion Ridge Press LLC

Mt Zion Ridge Press LLC
295 Gum Springs Rd, NW
Georgetown, TN 37366

https://www.mtzionridgepress.com

ISBN 13: 978-1-955838-28-3

Published in the United States of America
Publication Date: July 1, 2022

Copyright: © Bettie Boswell 2022
Editor-In-Chief: Michelle Levigne
Executive Editor: Tamera Lynn Kraft

Cover art design by Tamera Lynn Kraft

Cover Art Copyright by Mt Zion Ridge Press LLC © 2022

Dedication

To my husband David, our children and grandchildren, my critique partner, Ann Cavera, Antebellum Tour Guides of Columbus, MS (& Waverly Mansion), those who created a musical about The Free State of Winston, and buddies from Sylvania Historical Village experiences: Joy Armstrong, Joy Brown-Latimer, and Beth Jacobs. A big thank you to Tamera and Michelle for giving this book a home. Praise the Lord!

Prelude

Two Years before the production of *Incident at Woodson House*

Ginny Cline needed to write a musical. The problem was, she didn't know if she could find the courage to do it. She lugged the heavy carton full of historic material from her car and up the steps to her little yellow bungalow. Scents of ancient paper, leather, and the past wafted from the box as she leaned it against the doorframe and inserted her key. Jezebel's anxious woofs sounded from the laundry room where the basset hound spent her day.

It had been a long one for the dog and Ginny, the hound's fourth grade teacher owner. Ginny's stop by the Forest Glen Historical Museum to pick up the artifact-filled box had turned into a brainstorming marathon with curator Annie. The energetic woman urged Ginny to try writing a Broadway style musical about Woodson House, a local Underground Railroad station site. Who would have thought that writing a short musical for her school children a year ago would offer the opportunity to try her hand once again at creating a larger musical for the community? Only Annie could have come up with the farfetched idea. She was one of the few friends who knew about Ginny's disastrous attempt at writing a musical during her college years.

Ginny set the heavy box down on the floor and headed for her hound. When she opened Jezebel's door, the slobbery beast brushed past her and ran for the box. Jezebel sniffed, and then clamped her teeth around a leatherbound book as she tugged it from the box.

"Oh no you don't!" Ginny pried the volume from the dog's mouth and sent her outside. She transferred the box's contents to the top of the large oak desk she'd inherited from her grandmother and started sorting through memorabilia that the Woodson family descendants donated to the museum.

Annie's words from this morning sang in her ears like a siren luring her to answer the call. "We took a step in faith to add the Woodson House to the museum's holdings. Now our budget is out of whack. We need something to increase donations and draw attention to the museum and the Woodson house connection to the Underground Railroad. With your God-given talent, you could write a fundraising musical for us to use at the museum." She'd paused and grabbed Ginny's hands. "I know you wrote a musical when you were in college and things went bad. This will give you a chance to right or should I say 'write' that wrong. Maybe even allow you to be free to love someday."

The challenge to create had stirred Ginny's heart and given her the courage to at least try. When it came to the love connection, she'd answered with a firm no. She received plenty of love from her fourth graders. Jezebel's scratch at the door brought her thoughts back to the present. After letting the dog in and filling up a bowl with chow, she reached across the desk and retrieved a ribbon-bound leather volume with letters and clippings poking out from its yellowed pages. As she loosened the ribbon, a letter near the front of the book fluttered to the desk's top. The letter bore the date of February 15, 1858. Ginny studied the epistle and the open page of the journal. She picked up her pen and started jotting information in a spiralbound notebook. Casting away her doubts, her mind bubbled with ideas of what the musical might look like.

Woodson House, Forest Glen, Ohio
February 15, 1858

Dearest Matilda,

Our nieces are in trouble. Yes, there is more than one niece, but I suspect you knew of the possibility. It's time for you to assert yourself before the situation gets worse than it is already. The dear girls are maturing and our brother has taken on a new bride, along with her wayward son. My husband's nephew, Samuel, was passing through the south on a trip for the Cause. He attended our brother's nuptials in my stead and painted a grim picture of the danger our girls may be facing. I am enclosing Samuel's letter which describes the situation. I wish that one of us could have been there, but I understand you were still grieving your dear husband and attending to the last of your farm's business. Perhaps now, you will consider joining me in the north. We have several empty rooms now that our children are grown.

The widow Amanda and her son Sidney have a reputation among my southern contacts that does not bode well for the safety and health of either our brother or the girls. Since you are closer in proximity than I, please consider a visit, post haste. I fear that unless you take action the young women will be facing all manner of evil.

If you can convince our brother to allow our nieces a trip north to Woodson House, then we can make sure they find a way to live in the freedom they both deserve. I trust you will know what to do. There is a system of canals from north of Cincinnati to Toledo that pass not far from our Woodson House. Just beware of snakes along the way.

When we built our home, I had my husband build a little playroom, much like the dragon's den we used to have when we were small. The hidden room may provide a refuge for one of our nieces. I think you will understand when you meet the girls. If you and the young ladies do come north to live with me, you will find several features in my home bearing a resemblance to our old plantation estate, just not on such a grand dimension.

Your loving sister,
Mary Etta Woodson

Chapter 1

Holly Plantation-Western Alabama-March 1858

Early

Hairs rose on Early's arms. Something wasn't right. She paused in her ascent up the stairs to the plantation home's fourth floor cupola. Floorboards squeaked from the stairs below. The plantation home often creaked like an old man's joints when the weather changed, but she couldn't shake the feeling that tonight's groans were different. Another sound echoed in the stairwell. Did someone clear their throat? Warm air rose from the spacious rooms below, reminding her to resume her climb. Moisture broke out on her forehead.

Fear of the new mistress's hand spurred Early onward to her task. Once she opened the high cupola windows, the heat below would flow out, bringing cooling relief, hopefully before the family woke up in discomfort. Five more steps put her feet on the high landing surrounded by windows.

Swoosh. A breeze rushed out through the open portal. Early pushed the heavy window frame higher and moaned. One down. Three more to go. If only the feeling that someone watched her would go away. Shadows flickered across the landing as a gentle wind blew through the live oaks standing in silhouette against a full moon. Spanish moss wavered in the breeze, adding to her apprehension. Early stretched her back and shook off her fear. She had a job to do. If she did not open all the ventilating windows soon, the whole household would blame her, the slave girl who made them too warm during this early spring night. Push — another window. Pull — another window.

Crash!

An acrid smell like rotten apples filtered up from below, as the sound of glass from a breaking container tinkled down the curved stairway. Early peered over the mahogany railing and spotted her follower. He kicked his broken bottle to the side and grinned upwards. His face glowed with an eerie hue in the filtered moonlight.

"Hello my darlin', I've been lookin' for ya. I was gonna offer you a swig o' my drink but it looks like I dropped it." Master Hollings' new stepson, Sidney cackled as he stood in her only path to relative freedom.

He was two flights down. There was no way back to the servant's room under the kitchen. Early held back her panic with a clinched jaw and fled one floor down. She hoped against hope that Missy's door would be open.

"Are ya coming for me, my dark-skinned beauty?"

Early's moist hands fought for a firm grip on the doorknob. She swiped her hands on her dress and grabbed the knob again. *Please, Heavenly Father.* She tightened her hands and wrenched hard to the left. The door unlatched with a loud snap that rang in her ears. *Thank You, Lord.*

Faltering footsteps wove up the stairs as she clicked the door closed. Her hands shook. She fumbled for the key, which should be located in the inner keyhole. Good, it was there, the key to her safety. Early blew out a deep breath when locking pins clattered into place.

"What's going on here?" Her entrance roused young Mistress Hollings, who sat up in the high four-poster bed. Partial darkness and the mosquito netting surrounding the bed softened the dismayed look on Missy's face.

"Hide me, Missy. Please. I can't be found by that terrible man." Early trembled at her audacity, praying her life-long companion would overlook her disobedience. Would Missy's loyalty to her new mother take precedence over the friendship of the child whose mother had nursed them both? Would her young mistress heed her early morning call for help?

Missy adjusted the mobcap that held her ringlets in tight curls, waiting to be set free in the day to come. "Did you say something Early? What are you doing here in the middle of the night?" She laughed and added, "Perhaps I should have Papa flog you for interrupting my sound sleep."

The familiar teased threat filled Early with fear. She gaped in silence at her childhood companion. Was Missy joking, as she had when they where children, or did she offer a true threat? Life was different since Master Hollings had added a new wife and son to the household. Perhaps the relationship between the two young women would become another unwelcome casualty.

Missy parted her netted curtain and stepped onto the stool beside her bed. Early bowed her head as waves of terror filled her heart. "Early, are you all right?" The young mistress pulled a lacy handkerchief from her bedside table and dabbed it on her servant's tear-streaked face. "You know I'd never have you flogged, but you better tell me what is wrong."

Early swallowed, fighting the bile climbing up her throat as she swiped the pristine hankie across her cheeks. "I need your help, Missy. I'm scared he's going to hurt me. More scared than I've ever been in my life."

"Why should you be scared? I'm not going to let anyone hurt you. I've made Papa promise that you will always be mine. That's never going to change if I can help it."

Early fought against rising anger at the reminder of her position as a slave, but right now she needed help. "What if you can't protect me? I don't think I'm safe in this house anymore. That man tried to come after me tonight."

"What! Tell me who it was and I'll put an end to it this very minute."

Boom. Something crashed against the door to Missy's room. A muttered curse filtered through the door, followed by an out of tune chorus about a 'dark lass, with curling hair.' "Open the door, you pretty young thing. You can't hide from me forever."

Missy's gasped, "Sidney?" was answered by a terrified nod. Missy placed her hands on Early's shoulders. "Don't you worry, honey. Just wait until Papa and Mother Amanda get back from their trip. Amanda and strong drink have spoiled Sidney. I'll see that he answers to Papa."

A loud pounding at Missy's door sent both young women into each other's arms. The knob rattled but refused to give. Early gave thanks to the Lord that she had taken the time to turn the key.

"Come out from there, woman. I'm the new master of this house and I'll do what I want." A loud belch echoed in the hallway, followed by another thump against the door. The raucous tune rang through the solid barrier once more. Missy and Early listened in horror until the song faded into a loud snore.

Tension fell from Early's shoulders like a load of sopping wet bed linens. The rumbling snorts grew louder and settled into a restless pattern of snores. Sidney's rampage was over for the night but he still blocked any exit from the room. A drunken doorstop full of trouble...

"Do you want me to go, Missy?" Another wave of shivers shook Early as she peered at her mistress.

"You won't be able to get around that sleeping nuisance outside the door. Use the lounge on the balcony tonight. The fresh air will do you good." Missy's hug filled Early with warmth.

They jumped away from each other as different sounds arose. Low-pitched voices rumbled on the other side of the door. The two women crept closer to the noise. Missy placed her ear against the door to listen. Early slowly pulled the big key from its hole and peeked through to see what was happening. Two servants stood outside the door.

The ever-present Moses, head household slave and butler for the family, stood hunched over the sleeping stepson's form. She did not recognize the other man. As she watched him help the aging Moses pick up Sidney's drooping body, she couldn't help but admire the muscles that bulged from underneath his cotton shirt. Cinnamon-colored eyes seemed to pierce right through the keyhole when the brawny man turned her way. He shook his head and stared at the door with a sad expression. The invisible contact made her jump back from the door. Confusion shot through her as she placed a hand on her pounding heart.

"What's the matter, Early? What's going on now?" Missy quickly took her place at the peep hole. "Oh my... So who scares you more, my stepbrother or our new carriage driver?"

"Begging your pardon, Missy, but that's not funny considering what happened tonight." Early leaned against the door frame and glared at her mistress. Missy's caring eyes looked back. Confidence in the relationship with her old friend flowed into Early's wavering thoughts like a calming breeze.

"You're right. I'll see what Papa can do about the situation when he returns. Until this is resolved, you can stay here with me. The balcony lounge chaise is waiting for you." Missy held out the Dresden Plate quilt that usually lay folded across the end of her bed.

"Thank you, Missy." Early draped the patterned quilt across her shoulders and moved toward the balcony. She pushed up the first section of windowpanes that had been lowered earlier during the late evening. Mild night air filled her lungs. It only took a few more seconds to unlatch the jib doorway at the bottom of the window, which opened up a path to the small balcony hovering over the garden below.

A short while later, Missy's deep breathing from inside the house reached Early's ears as she settled on the cushioned wicker lounge chair. Normally the night sounds of another sleeping human didn't affect her. Heaven knew that old Nellie's snores shook the rafters in the cellar room where they slept. The old woman's rumbles hadn't ceased tonight when Early awakened to make her trip up the stairs. Even though warmth filled the air, she shivered and sank into the lounge, wrapping the quilt around her shoulders.

Life had been so much simpler before Sidney's arrival. It was almost as if she and Missy were real sisters, except for the chores. Nevertheless, that was the way things had always been. This was the life she knew, and before recent events most days had been fairly pleasant. Sure, there were a few times, as a child, when she felt jealous of her own mother's attention to the master's young daughter. Mama had explained that she loved Early best. The answer had been good enough for the young girl who knew no other life.

Tonight she questioned everything she had known. Was she really safe? Confusion over her real relationship to the young woman snoozing in the high-netted bed just inside the large plantation home left questions in her mind. Would she survive if the master or his new wife removed her from the prized maid position and made her work in the fields? She'd encountered a few field hands who had mocked her with words saying she wouldn't last a day working cotton.

She gazed at the star-filled sky and wondered if the tales were true about following the drinking gourd to Canaan Land. She knew in her heart that someday, when she breathed her last earthly breath, her Heavenly Father would carry her off to Canaan. She'd heard talk that there was a Canaan here in this world. Some people called it Canada.

According to Master Hollings, no one would ever want to live in Canada. Tales of frozen barren land where crops would not grow made her think she never wanted to go there. However, would it be worth it if she didn't have to deal with Sidney? Even more important, would it be worth going there if it involved traveling with a handsome cinnamon-eyed man riding a charging stallion? Drifting into a sleep fraught with nightmares and hopes, Early tossed and turned before finally falling into an exhausted slumber.

Missy

Missy controlled her breathing, making it as even as the cooling breeze flowing in the window. Once she heard Early's breath slow into a rhythmic pattern on the balcony, she allowed her anger to churn like waves in a storm. Clutching her pillow close to her chest, she stifled a frustrated cry of disgust. When Sidney moved to Holly Plantation after Papa's marriage, her repulsion had fought with jealousy. Papa seemed blind to the young man's imperfections, which revealed themselves in an ugly way tonight with his threats toward Early. She'd endured a few of his leering gazes herself, but so far he hadn't chased her like he did with her maid.

She flopped to her other side and huffed out a breath that blew the mosquito netting in a ghostly wave. Her desire to do something warred with the fact that she had no power to free Early, or any other slaves for that matter. Papa had started hinting he needed a male heir, saying Missy would find her place on another plantation with an influential owner. No man on neighboring plantations appealed to her. The only male who even stirred her heart in the least had only been passing through the south. Chances were she would never see him again. Papa certainly would never approve her interest in a northern man. Instead, her father recently dared to suggest Sidney as a suitor. Even before tonight she had no use for the disgusting man, whom Papa said could provide for her every need.

Material possessions filled her room, all supplied by the labor of others. She resisted the temptation to get up and shred her hooped skirts and fancy baubles into rags before the sun rose. Destroying them would only cause her doting papa to provide more goods, at the expense of slave labor. She rolled out of the bed and tiptoed to her desk. Feeling the carved surface beneath her hands, she popped open a hidden drawer filled with treasures. Her fingers carefully traced smooth stones from a broken necklace, bird feathers, her mother's tattered Bible, and the book her Ohio uncle's nephew had quietly slipped into her possession at the wedding. The warning to keep it hidden from prying eyes had sent a tingle down her spine as their hands touched and she'd looked into his intense blue eyes. She carried the handsome young man's treasured book to her bed and tucked it under her pillow. Maybe it was time to further unravel the volume's mysteries, as soon as morning light arrived. He'd asked her to keep it hidden, with a warning. Having the book in her possession would cause trouble if someone found it.

Tangled covers immobilized her body as the night dragged on like a turtle. Sleep didn't come. She pulled the book from beneath her feather pillow and fingered the tattered pages. A paper fell from the tome. She knew without looking that the parchment offered a name, an address, and a dare to use her gift of poetry in the fight for freedom. Samuel, the nephew of her Aunt Mary Etta's husband had placed it there with his challenge.

He'd come to represent their aunt's family at Papa's wedding to Amanda. His handsome eyes had followed Missy from across the room and connected with hers for a moment before he shook his head and looked away. His reaction had seemed strange since most young men wanted to come closer and introduce themselves to any available young women. Her confusion rose like a twisted vine when Samuel stared in abhorrence and pity at Moses and Early when Sidney complained to them about their service. Samuel's disgusted gaze had followed the two servants as they carried trays of refreshments around the parlor for the wedding guests to enjoy. Missy confronted him and discovered his distaste for slavery.

When she indicated her own dislike and inability to change things, she discovered Samuel worked for an anti-slavery newspaper. They had moved their conversation to a quiet corner, where he admitted to enjoying the poetry she recited at the wedding. He'd shared that he sometimes published poetry in his newspaper. His interest touched something deep inside her soul and the memory lingered long after he left.

Later that same evening when they danced at the wedding reception, he had challenged her to write a poem for his paper. Did she dare? She'd heard of pen names. That might be a safe way to express her thoughts and not face Papa's wrath. Did she have the strength to defy her own flesh and blood? Doubt and defiance fought a battle in her mind.

Papa had been angry the next morning when he discovered Samuel whispering with some of the slaves. The young man departed soon afterwards with Papa's glare following him. His parting salutation had been a wave when he spotted her standing on the front porch. Her gaze had followed him as his horse carried him down the lane and away from Holly Plantation.

She pulled his book close to her chest and held it there until she replaced it securely under her pillow. Rereading it in the morning might provide her with some much needed inspiration. She'd always enjoyed writing. Papa had even given her a thick journal and the special Thoreau pencils as part of the wedding festivities. Not long after the young man left, she'd drawn a sketch of Samuel, using the softest pencil from the set. She also wrote a short poem about a dark-haired cavalier with shining blue eyes. The gleam in his eyes had challenged her to use her writing skill in a way she'd never thought of before. Perhaps her words could find wings like those in his well-worn volume. Maybe she could do more than compose love songs in the nearly new journal.

~~~~~

Hours later, Missy untangled the light counterpane that encased her body after the endless night of tossing and turning. Thankfulness for a safe night warred with anger. Everything had changed since the wedding. Her father seemed distant and blindly devoted to his new wife and Sidney. How could he not see that Sidney posed a danger to Early and his own daughter? She clamped her eyes closed as she heard sounds coming from the balcony. The soft padding of Early's feet and click of a closing door caused Missy to crack open her weighted eyelids. Even her relationship with Early had changed. Playmate, companion, confidant and now, thanks to stepmother Amanda, recognition as a true slave...

She pulled the book from under her pillow and studied several
~~~~~

pages that were marked with a strand of embroidery thread. Bright beams of morning sunlight highlighted words that opened her eyes to the horrors most people in slavery endured. Maybe her words could make a difference, like those in the book. Sliding out of the tall bed, Missy shuffled her way across the carpeted floor and moved the journal, a quill, and a bottle of ink into position on the pulled down secretary desk. She opened the journal to her sketch of the handsome man who smiled back at her. Courage filled her heart as she imagined him nodding his head in approval. Flipping to a blank sheet of paper, she dipped the nib of her feathered pen into berry-colored ink and paused above the page. A drop of ink fell to the white surface. She blotted it up. Inspiration hit.

> *Slavery blots our history,*
> *A dark mark on this land so free.*
>
> *Some have rights, while others bleed,*
> *Forced to meet another's need.*
>
> *There was no choice to serve this way,*
> *When brought from homelands, far away.*
>
> *Now they're forced against their will,*
> *To labor long and share pig swill,*
>
> *How long will God look on this land,*
> *Unless we take a stubborn stand?*

After finishing her poem, Missy penned the events of the night before into her leatherbound journal, which her papa had given her. She felt a slight twinge of betrayal, knowing she used Papa's gift to record the horrors of slavery. He had traveled to Amanda's hometown several times before the marriage and he'd picked up the journal on his final trip there. More poem ideas to share with her aunt's nephew swirled through her head. She turned to a new page in the journal and poured out her heart with ink. She switched to a number two pencil when her ink supply diminished. She only took a break for a few moments when Early brought a breakfast tray. The food grew cold as she continued writing.

A commotion outside her open window broke into her jottings. She scurried to peer out and watched several house servants carry in packages.

"Welcome home Papa!" She leaned out the window and started to say more, but Amanda frowned and shook her head as she stepped from the carriage. Her stepmother disappeared into the house while Papa talked to the new groomsman.

The horse tender bowed his head and turned to the team. She watched as the younger man bent over and lifted the hoof on one of Papa's matched bays. He patted the mare's rump and assisted an older man as they led the carriage and team toward the barn. Too bad Early wasn't around to spy on the new man. At least Papa was home. Maybe she could convince him to see Sidney's weakness for women and wine.

A tap on the door brought Missy's thoughts to a halt when she heard her stepmother's voice. "May I come in Melissa?"

"One moment, ma'am." Missy stepped closer to the desk and closed it. She pulled a wrapper around her nightclothes before she invited her stepmother to enter.

"We picked up the post on our way through town. It seems you have a letter from your aunt." The chill in Amanda's voice froze Missy's thoughts as she wondered if Uncle's nephew Samuel had dared to write through their mutual aunt. The broken seal spoke of prying eyes.

Aunt 'Tilda's name and address on the envelope brought a sigh of relief. Her aunt from northern Alabama had visited when Missy was smaller, bringing joy and entertaining stories of hill country life.

"It seems we are having company soon. I will need your slave girl to leave your side for a while and help with the preparations."

"Yes ma'am." Missy took the letter and curtsied to her stepmother.

Where had her gumption gone? She swallowed and placed her hands on her hips. "But not today, I have errands to run and I need Early to attend me."

"You spoil the girl. That needs to change, along with your manners. Yelling out the window does not befit the way a young lady of your standing should behave. Your father and I will be making some adjustments after we get back from our trip to my sister's plantation. We're leaving again later today, but know that your life, and your maid's, will be different when we get back." Amanda's lips flattened as she floated out of the room with her head held high.

Missy opened the missive and sat down on the edge of her bed to read.

Winston County (formerly Hancock,) Alabama
February 27, 1858

Dearest Melissa,

You may not remember me well, but I am your father's sister and your aunt. I think when I last saw you, you were but a tot. Your Papa has written me many good things about you, including the fact that you are going by the name Missy, when you were given the beautiful birth name Melissa. Wear your name proudly, my dear, it was a gift from your loving mother. She was a sweet soul, may she rest in God's peace.

I must apologize for not making the trip to witness the matrimonial vows your father Arthur spoke to your stepmother Amanda. However, your Aunt Mary Etta has informed me of the details through a letter she wrote, after her husband's nephew returned to her beloved Ohio. You seem to have made a lasting impression on the young man.

She had other news which I will share with you when I do manage to make a visit down your way. I plan to be there within the next month. I will send a message to your Papa through the telegraph operators once I finalize my business here in Winston County.

I would welcome the chance to take you on a little carriage ride adventure, your father permitting. It is high time you saw a bit of the world outside of your sheltered life at the plantation. I am not an advocate of slavery but I beg you to consider bringing along your personal servant. My fingers are getting a little arthritic these days and I fear I could never do the corsets and buttons of a young woman justice. I much prefer a simpler dress style which has proven to be helpful as the widow of a hill country farmer. Your father wrote that you have a deep attachment to the girl. I suppose I will indeed have to make a concession to having you bring along one bound in slavery, if your father agrees to let you travel.

Yours Truly,
Aunt Matilda Hollings McCallum

Missy opened the desk and pulled some writing paper from a stack provided for correspondence. Much to her delight, she discovered another container of ink. Perfect. She copied her best poems onto the fresh paper and after they dried, folded them into an envelope. It was time she wrote a letter of her own.

Dear Samuel Woodson,

Please pardon my boldness but I have decided to act upon your challenge. At my Papa's wedding you dared me to make a difference. I am seeing more evidence of the cruelty around me and will attempt to send you some words that may help you with the cause against those evils. In some ways I fear for my own well being, so I request that you publish my works anonymously. I do not have your courage to stand boldly on my own. Because of that, I ask that you do not respond to me about this matter since my private letters have shown evidence of tampering by others. I have faith that you will only use articles which are appropriate and helpful. In today's letter, please find several pieces for your consideration, knowing that I understand I will not be hearing from you regarding this matter.

Sincerely,
Melissa Hollings

Missy blew the letter's ink dry, not daring to blot it and leave any impression of her correspondence. Her fingers itched to write more. She retrieved one of her earlier poems and turned the page over. Light from her window brightened the paper; a streak of light inspired her to dip the pen in dark ink. The scratch of each pen stroke brought satisfaction and peace along with an element of daring as she broke from standard poetic forms.

Darkness and Light

Raised in the darkness of ignorance, I saw no other way.
Like scripture I began to see the cloudy reflection in the eyes of
those around me.
Eyes half shuttered by obedience yet seeking something more:
Freedom, hope, a life beyond what we force upon them.

Shards of light in my darkened world until I'm made to see,
The life we live keeps us from being free.
The messenger who came to me has pierced my clouded eyes
And opened up a ray of light.

What can I do to have my say?
I know no other way of life,
A child whose roots are in the south, trained in poetry.
To paint and play and let them wait on me.

I look around. I know it's wrong. The image now is clear.
I cannot march against my world but I can write a song.
A song of words, much like a sword, inspiring acts I dare not
do,
Stirring those who have the strength to take my place instead.

I'll gird their armor on with ink, with feathered slash and stab.
A shaft of light in our dark world to show our ways must
change,
I will rearrange the world I know.
Lord, help me share my feelings and the things I see each day.

Please let these words give someone strength and hope of
freedom's light.

She paused and heard Amanda's bossy voice filter up the stairs. She'd managed to commandeer some of Early's time, regardless of Missy's wishes. The sound of a slap followed a tirade and she flinched at her maid's cry. Anger coursed into her fingers. She lifted her feather and then dropped it into the ink as another thought filtered through her mind.

My Sister in Chains

My darker skinned sister, companion and friend,
I'm told is my slave and I don't comprehend.
My eyes have been opened to what that can be,
To live life in fear of the whip on bowed knee.

Or work without wages until life is done,
In a sweltering kitchen, or field in the sun.
Guilt fills my mind as my needs are all met
By this darker skinned woman in slavery, and yet...

She's more like a sister for most of the day,
When others are present life's more like a play.
We put on an act of mistress and maid,
Seeking a way to stay unafraid.

No life is our own,
Though I sit on a throne.
While my sister who's brown,
Serves us all with no frown.

Though mocked by new kin,
She holds harsh words within.
Looks down at her feet,
So eyes do not meet.

The people in charge,
Of our fates small or large.
Help me stand on my feet,
Not fall in defeat.

Can I leave this behind
Take whatever I find
In a world with none bound
Where we might be found?

Missy smiled with satisfaction as she sealed the envelope and tucked it into her reticule. The trip to town would serve more than one purpose today. Feeling a little guilty, she called Early to help her get ready for the day. There was no way she could get into her corset without help.

Early

Early tugged on Missy's corset strings, which cinched an already narrow waist. She heard her mistress gasp.

"Ouch, I think this is tight enough. So — I'm thinking — umph — that while Sidney is indisposed, it might be a good time for me to take a carriage ride to town."

Early knotted the corset strings. The tightness in her chest pinched worse than her mistress's secured waist. Terror raced through her thoughts. She would be without Missy's protection. She crossed her arms to keep from shaking. "I'm sure you would enjoy the ride, but if you don't mind, may I stay locked up in your room or even better hide me in our old playroom in the cellar."

"I certainly do mind. I want you to come with me today. I don't think you have to worry about my stepbrother this morning. He is sure to be asleep after his rampage last night." Missy raised her hands as Early draped a fresh dress over her head and spread it over ruffled petticoats. "I got a letter from Aunt 'Tilda this morning and I want to get something new to wear while she visits. She even hinted about taking us on an extended trip in a carriage."

"But Missy, I don't think I've ever been out in the carriage before. Mama and I lived in the room under the kitchen for as long as she was alive. Now it's me and Nellie down there. I've never been any further than some of the quarters down past the barn. I don't think I'd know what to do in a carriage." Nor would she know what to do if a certain young man was working with the horses.

"Sure you would, Early. You just have to sit there and enjoy the ride. You might even see something you like." Missy's mischievous grin warned Early that her thoughts were on more than just magnolia trees and spring blossoms.

Visions of the handsome new carriage driver's muscular body and warm eyes danced through Early's mind as she fumbled with the buttons of her mistress's dress. "It might be nice to see the countryside, and other things."

"That's what I thought. Now, let's finish up here and get ready for a day in town. It's high time I showed you about life outside this plantation." Missy's expression seemed different as she peered deeply into Early's eyes.

Early glanced down, a strange feeling coursed through her chest. Her fingers fumbled as she huddled at Missy's feet, hooking the fasteners on kid leather boots. Worried thoughts of Missy's new stepbrother marched across her mind, regardless of her mistress's assurances. This trip could be wonderful or it could turn into a terrible disaster.

Chapter Two

George

George loosened the tight collar of his carriage driver's livery. As he watched the women approach, he found his eyes straying to the mistress's girl. The short young woman wore a dark dress, befitting her role as house servant, which contrasted with her honey-colored skin. His hands gripped the reins tighter as his thoughts turned to the night before. Moses mentioned he saw the maid sneaking from Missy's room this morning. If that snake hadn't been drunk, or the young woman so helpful, who knows what would have happened to the appealing woman. Not that he cared. She probably thought herself better than the people who worked outside of the big house.

"Here you go, Miss." Moses gently assisted young Mistress Hollings into the cushioned leather seat of the family's open phaeton. Her quiet servant stood nearby and waited for Moses' assistance. She wore a confused expression as the elderly servant led her to the front of the carriage and whispered, "It's not proper for you to sit with your mistress. You'll have to sit up here with the driver since there isn't a boot in this carriage."

"A boot? Why would a carriage need a shoe?" Her melodic voice rang in George's ears.

He chuckled as Moses explained, "A boot is not a shoe. It's a small seat where footmen sometimes sit in a larger carriage."

"Footman? Never mind. I'm sorry. I've never been out for a ride before." She peered up to where George sat and gasped. He couldn't resist doffing his felt hat as he stared into hazel-tinted eyes. She stumbled into Moses as she neared the small ladder leading to the high front seat. Her head tipped backward. She eyed the high steps and swallowed.

"Allow me to help, Miss." Moses' voice broke whatever trance she'd escaped into.

Taking the older man's weathered hand in her left one, she stretched her other arm toward a rung on the carriage's ladder.

George reached down, his large hand engulfing her tiny one. He easily lifted her onto the seat next to him. A jolt of awareness coursed through him as he hesitantly let go of her hand. She stiffened beside him and looked away. Just as he thought, she didn't want to get dirt from the barn or from him on her, so she held herself aloof.

Moses laughed as she looked down from her perch. "Have a good day, Miss Early. I'm thinking you're gonna enjoy your first ride with our new driver." The patriarch saluted and winked. George nodded as he released the brake and gathered the reins in his gloved hands.

He began to whistle a spiritual about crossing the river. He needed to center his thoughts on something other than the stuck up little filly who sat beside him. Someday he was going to gallop across the Jordan into Canaan land and he didn't need anyone or anything holding him back. As his tune soared into the air, his seatmate seemed to relax. He glanced her way and noticed she mouthed the words about crossing over the Jordan to be with the Lord. Maybe she wasn't so above him after all.

"So Miss Early, this is your first ride." George couldn't resist a wink of his own as the young house servant suddenly tensed and nervously glanced his way. Her shy nod shook one of her braids loose from the simple calico bonnet she wore over her raven black hair. "Don't worry. I've been driving since I was ten years old. I've never met a horse that didn't like me. Just sit back and leave the driving to good old George."

"So you're old, are you? I wouldn't have guessed that you were more than a few days past twenty."

"Well, maybe I am and maybe I'm not. I have to be older than you are anyways. You look like a fresh faced little girl, to me." George could not resist a smile as she opened up to his conversation.

"I'll have you know that I'm seventeen years old, as near as I can tell. Besides, Missy says it's not nice to ask a lady her age." Early straightened her bonnet and pushed the wayward hair back into place.

"Do you believe everything that Missy tells you?" George heard the sarcasm in his voice and wondered if he had overstepped a boundary.

"Sure I do. She loves me and takes care of me." Early pressed her skirt with delicate hands and looked at the road ahead.

George ruefully shook his head. "That's because you do everything she tells you to do. Someday you'll do something wrong. Then things will change like they did for me."

She reached over to lay a comforting hand over George's arm and then snatched it away. "What do you mean by that?"

"My whole family worked with the horses on a plantation in Maryland. Then the master got a new foreman who forced other black people to act as spies. Seems they did not like my sense of humor. Now I will never see my family again." George tightened his hands on the reins as he resisted the urge to say more.

Silence met his reply before Early answered. "I've heard of such things but nothing like that ever happened to me. My mama was like a mother to Missy. When she passed away from malaria a few years ago, we both mourned her passing. Just like any daughters would have done."

Sorrow and a tinge of jealousy filled George's heart as he urged the horses to trot a little faster. Edging closer to Early, he spoke in a whisper. "One of these days I'm gonna hitch my horses to old Moses' chariot and take a ride up north."

"What are you talking about George? I didn't know Moses had any chariots back at our place." She turned her face and beautiful hazel eyes looked his way.

"Hush. You are such an innocent. I'm not talking about your Moses back there in the house. I'm talking about the Moses that's gonna take us to the Promised Land. At least she did that back in Maryland. I can only hope there's someone like her here in Alabama."

"I thought Jesus would take us to the Promised Land, not Moses."

"Yeah, maybe He can or maybe He can't do that, but I'm talking about another Moses, one that traveled around Maryland. I heard there could be someone like her around here. There was a young man from Ohio who came to the big wedding. He hinted that there might be a Moses coming with the springtime."

"Now you've really got me confused. How can Moses be a woman?" Early's frustrated sigh reached back to Missy as the carriage slowed to take a turn toward town.

"Hello you two," Missy called out from behind them. "Are you having a good conversation up there?"

"We were just talking about—ouch."

George gave Early a swift knee jab as he took over the conversation. "Beg your pardon, Miss, but did you notice a herd of deer over there in the edge of the forest?" He pointed to a glade of trees.

Missy and Early both searched for the deer but found none where he pointed. When Early turned to George with a puzzled look on her face, he frowned and held a finger to pursed lips. Missy just giggled and raised questioning eyebrows before she lowered her focus to her journal, where she scratched pencil marks. Early silently faced forward. George drew in a tight breath and hoped that he had not revealed too much to the woman, who both intrigued and scared him to death.

Early

The busyness of the crowded town's streets both scared and amazed Early as they drove down the main avenue edged with brick and white clapboard homes and storefronts. Only the dust from the road kept Early from gaping at the stores and throngs of people. A rainbow of wide, colorful skirts contrasted with the dark hues of men's coats and trousers, as townspeople greeted her mistress.

Missy waved to several and then clapped her hands. "Driver, please stop here. I want to visit the milliner's for a moment. I just saw the most beautiful hat in the window." She threw herself to the edge of her seat and pointed to a nearby shop. Early watched as George slowed the horses and pulled to the side of the street. He tied the reins off and pulled the brake lever in place. As he performed each movement, he explained his actions to Early.

Her heart beat an irregular rhythm when he easily jumped off the side of the carriage. Then he bowed before Missy, offering assistance as she stepped down. The young mistress shaded her eyes and looked up.

"Miss Early, will you be coming in with me or staying here with your new friend?"

Early grinned at Missy's friendly comment and couldn't resist a tease of her own. "Oh Missy, do you think I need to replace my bonnet with something better?"

Several passing faces, both white and brown, stopped to stare at the young slave and her mistress. George quickly stepped into the line of sight between the two young women. "Begging your pardon, Miss, I will take care of your girl while you look for a new hat."

Missy laughed and flounced toward the merchant. Anger grew like a flame in Early's chest. She tried to pray for a calm spirit. It didn't help. Fire shot through her as she hissed, "How dare you order me around like that, you — you — man."

His lips flattened as he leaned close and whispered a response that shook her world. "You're a slave. You can't talk to your mistress that way in public. It will get you both in big trouble if you're not careful."

"But Missy and I are like sisters. It's not like that at all. We were raised together."

"Didn't you see those people on the street? They were all surprised. It will be a miracle if none of them report you to the master." Worry lines wrinkled his brow.

"I believe in miracles, George, so I'm going to trust in God to take care of me." Early straightened her backbone and scooted to the far end of the short carriage bench.

"I hope you are right because it will be a miracle if nothing happens. Now you open up your ears and listen to me. While we're in town you better be as quiet as a mouse."

"Mice aren't that quiet."

George rubbed his hand across his face before continuing. "Can you just listen? Don't say anything else that will draw attention to you or Missy. Maybe we'll get out of this without too much trouble."

Her defiant hazel eyes met pleading cinnamon ones and for a moment, there seemed to be a deep connection, causing Early to shudder and then wearily drop her attention to her hands. She gave a reluctant nod. George's shoulders relaxed and he leaned closer. His softened voice filled Early's ears as he told about each building in the block where their carriage stood.

"See that blacksmith shop over there? It's owned by a free man of color."

"Really?" Her jaw dropped open in awe as she contemplated the idea of someone of color living in freedom. "How is that possible?"

"Some masters allow their people to buy freedom." He brushed a fly away from his arm and stared up at the blue sky.

"I have never heard of a person of our race owning property. Tell me more of your tales." She shook her head in disbelief.

George continued to relate stories of his adventures in the place where he had lived as a child. He straightened with pride when he talked about some of the prize race horses he helped train for his former master. When he related the story of how his father had made him, as a youngster of twelve years of age, responsible for a pair of matched chestnut horses, his shoulders slumped. Emotion crackled its way into his voice as he told her how much he missed his family and the horses he cared for during his youth.

All too soon, Missy emerged from the milliner's shop carrying two hat cases. George sprang to her aid with a gentle manner and forced smile.

"I hope you don't mind, Early. I did see the perfect new bonnet for you." Missy nodded to one of the round boxes as she settled her skirts into place.

Early raised her eyebrows and gave George an 'I told you so' look. He briefly shook his head and frowned. After climbing back to the high seat, his eyes focused on something in the distance. His frown deepened. Her grin sagged as she turned to see what distraction had caught his attention.

George

George tensed. Anger twisted his gut when he noticed a sweat-flecked horse carrying a familiar rider, galloping down the road at a neck-breaking speed. As the quivering horse drew closer, the whites of its eyes revealed fear. The urge to teach the reckless rider a thing or two coursed into his fists. If only...

"Greetings, sister. Looks like you have a fine set of escorts today." Sidney's bloodshot eyes roamed over Early, who now huddled against George on the high seat. He forced his fists to relax and hoped she would feel safe.

Missy's demeanor changed swiftly in reaction to the arrival of the lanky young man whose breath still reeked of a night spent with more than one bottle of strong spirits. "I'm your stepsister, and I will not have you looking at Early that way."

"The last time I checked we live in a free country, unless you're a slave like those two."

Sidney's sneering laughter reignited George's anger but he held his thoughts to himself, choosing to look down at the horses. The carriage team and the abused mare all nervously pranced in reaction to Sidney's loud proclamations. Past consequences told him fighting back was not worth it. Someday that would change and he concentrated on thinking of the day he would catch a freedom train headed for the North. Forcing himself to breathe evenly seemed to have the desired effect on the petite shaking female leaning into his side, as she drew in a lung full of air.

"Well she's *my* slave and you will have nothing to do with her."

Early's body jerked beside him as she reacted to Missy's harshly spoken words. He reached for her hand and gave a quick squeeze. Her quiet tears began to flow in earnest as Sidney focused his counterattack on Missy.

"Maybe she is for now, but one of these days I'll be master of Holly Plantation and then we'll see what happens." Sidney's mare sidestepped and pawed the ground as her rider jerked the reins tight.

"Not if I can help it. I'll be talking this over with my father when he gets home. We'll see how he reacts to last night's events." Missy glared at her stepbrother and then turned her face away. "Driver, let's head for home. I think we're done here."

"We'll see about that, little sister." Wheeling his steed toward a nearby tavern, Sidney gave the horse's rump a sharp lash with the whip and nearly unseated himself as the animal reared in pain. "Behave, you stupid animal. You better obey me or I'll be trading you off like an unruly slave."

As the dust cleared, George gently squeezed Early's trembling forearm before he released the brake and headed the carriage for home. Silence engulfed the three young people, each reflecting on their own reaction to the scene that had played out in the town.

George shook his head and muttered, "I hope things don't get worse."

Chapter Three

Missy

Missy smoothed her skirts as she pushed the hat boxes and her reticule to the side. The crinkle of the hidden envelope reached her ears. She'd forgotten to mail the letter. Maybe it was just as well. Her fear of Sidney warred with the desire to make a difference. Maybe she could give her poetry to Aunt 'Tilda, or should she say Matilda since the woman wanted Missy to start going by her own given name. Her aunt had mentioned a dislike of slavery. She might be an advocate and a skirt to hide behind if things got difficult. She laced her fingers together to keep her hands steady. She needed to stay strong.

The carriage rocked from side to side, causing the couple in front of her to slide closer to each other. They'd been mighty quiet since leaving town. Early fit quite well against the side of the new driver. When she had peeked out of the milliner's window, the two seemed to be enjoying each other's company. Happiness had blossomed in her maid's cheeks when she had seemed enthralled by his conversation. That glow flew away like a bird in flight when Sidney showed up.

Missy huffed and focused on the countryside surrounding the path back to Holly Plantation. Fields of laborers hoed the ground, their backs bent as they worked. What would it be like to do that day after day with the only reward a mat on the floor and something to eat? Did Papa make sure his slaves had enough to fill their bellies each day? She squirmed in her seat as she noticed how thin the driver's frame was, compared to her own and Early's. Would she do better to share her poems with Papa and make a difference here? Words fluttered like an elusive butterfly as she fought to memorize her thoughts.

> *Endless days,*
> *Endless chores,*
> *Endless while the master snores.*

Clear the ground,
Plant the seeds,
Try to meet the master's needs.

Sew the dress,
Mend the suit,
Process master's canning fruit.

Fill the table,
Clean the plate,
Do it now and don't be late.

Missy cringed as she thought of the times she'd been irritated by a late dinner or a dress that didn't quite fit her figure. What had she done? Why did she even want to continue with the charade? Her journal tonight would be filled with disgust for the life she lived. If only her words could someday make a difference.

Ginny Interlude

Ginny flipped between the ancient journal filled with poetic thoughts and the letters inserted throughout its pages. All the information she'd discovered so far provided few details about Woodson House, other than the aunt's letter. Missy's record of her own beginning attraction and the one between Early and George did appeal to her romantic heart, broken long ago by the man who had stolen credit for the musical she wrote in college. She stretched and bent over to rub Jezebel, whose furry head and long ears caressed Ginny's bare toes. Warmth flowed from the hound's unconscious gesture. A little romance would add to the appeal of the musical. She turned to her computer and began to input words that seemed to flow from the Creator, to her soul.

How can I love when I'm not free to choose?
Offer you hope when there's so much to lose,
Only the Lord could change how we now live
He knows our hearts and the love we can give.

Our lives may be bound by the chains of a curse,

Forced to work hard, face pain, even worse,
But no man can own what you hold in your heart,
Love is from God, He won't keep us apart.

Ginny filled several pages with her thoughts before turning back to Missy's journal. She hoped she could do the story justice but a wave of doubt threatened her confidence. At least she had the freedom to choose someone to date, unlike the young women in the journal.

Early

A week later, Papa Hollings and his bride returned from their brief trip to her sister's plantation. Cargo wagons soon arrived with more goods purchased on their travels. The master had traded some of his profits, from last year's cotton, for silk material to dress his women in the finest. It seemed like the new Mrs. Hollings had brought home trinkets from all around the world. The whole household bustled as Amanda directed each parcel to be placed in the correct room.

Early carried the luxurious materials up the stairs and sighed in frustration. Sewing cotton fabrics had never been her favorite chore. Even with that softer fabric, she'd had to redo more than one seam and pricked her fingers many times in the process. She could only imagine the frustration of working with the new cloth. The slick texture of the silk would be a tricky challenge. She'd attempt to sew the material into an acceptable garment, because she had no other choice. Her mama often told her not to work up a mountain of worry over things out of her control. Missy had always been tolerant with sewing errors, but she doubted the new mistress would overlook even the simplest mistakes.

Leaving the fabric in Amanda's chambers, she scurried back downstairs to help other maids and men servants carry in blanket-wrapped china and statues. The new missus brought plenty of decorations to keep the slaves busy dusting and cleaning. Dusting wasn't her favorite chore but it could be relaxing. At least she'd enjoy looking over the new treasures. She took a flowered teacup from its wrapping and lifted it toward a window. The light revealed a shadow of her hand through the smooth surface. The china was high quality and expensive. Missy had taught her to recognize the finer things in life.

~~~~~

Three days later, Early positioned herself in the hallway, pretending to dust a marble figurine of a goddess. Her dust cloth fell to the ground as Missy entered her father's smoke-filled library. She picked up the rag and leaned closer to hear every word of her mistress's conversation through the open door. Missy had promised action, but would her longtime friend have the courage to follow through? She edged closer.

"Papa, I'm really concerned about Sidney's bothersome interest in Early. We both felt uncomfortable the night he chased her into my room." Missy's voice held a surprising amount of strength.

Master Hollings cleared his throat before replying, "Surely you are exaggerating, Missy. I only see an ambitious young man, who seems to have a taste for good wine. Perhaps he just had a little too much to drink."

"Papa, please listen to me. I'm really worried about the way Sidney acts when he's around her. It's not right."

Early pictured her friend stomping a foot as she spoke.

"It's just the way young men are, Missy. You'll understand yourself one day when you have a household of your own. Perhaps you are jealous of the fellow. After all, he isn't your blood brother. Nothing would make me happier than to see you take an interest in Sidney. That way there would never be any question about who should inherit this estate once his mother and I have gone on from this world." A racking cough rasped through the air and then Early heard the decorative tobacco tin open, signaling a refill for the Master's pipe.

"I do wish you would give up smoking that smelly leaf, Papa. I sometimes wonder if it isn't what is making you cough so much."

"I'll be fine, daughter. Now can we talk about more pleasant subjects? Your stepmother Amanda heard from some gossip that you purchased several hats on a recent trip to town."

"I have one hat, Papa. The other was a bonnet for Early. I thought she could use it to brighten her day."

"You purchased a milliner's hat for a slave? Perhaps things do need to change around here. You've babied that girl for far too long." Early heard a fist pound on the grand mahogany desk,
~~~~~

gracing the book-filled room. "Perhaps Amanda is right about how you favor your slave too much."

"But Papa, she's been like a sister to me and you know it. If her mother hadn't taken care of both of us from our infancy, I wouldn't have survived. You never had a problem with my relationship with Early, until Amanda and Sidney arrived."

"Enough of this talk. I'll think about your concerns, but in the meantime I better not hear of any impudence from your slave girl, unless you want me to sell her off or put her to work in the fields. I am the master of this house and my word will be final."

"Yes, Father." Missy slipped from the library, and spotting Early, pulled her down the hall. "You heard?"

"Yes, ma'am." Early fought back tears and resigned herself to her fate. Climbing the stairs to Missy's room took every drop of energy as she trudged up the curved staircase, dusting as she followed her mistress's steps. She bent her head toward the floor as she entered Missy's room on quiet feet.

"Early, come over here right now and talk to me." Missy flounced onto her settee and indicated her maid should use the embroidered chair sitting on the other side of the tea table. Without her usual bounce, Early approached her mistress with a bent head.

"What is wrong with you, Early? You don't seem like yourself these days."

Tears brimmed at the edge of her eyes as Early dared to look up at her mistress. "I guess I finally realized that I truly am a slave."

"What's the matter with that, as long as you have me for your friend?"

"But you're my owner so how can you be my friend, too?" Early's boldness returned as she crossed her arms and studied Missy's face. "Besides, what will become of me if something does happen to Master Hollings? Your snake of a stepbrother will be breathing down my neck and doing all kinds of evil things to me. I had a long talk with old Nellie about men the other day. I'm mighty scared of what could happen to me."

"Don't worry your sweet soul over our relationship. We'll just have to pray to God that the two of us will be together forever."

"What if the master has ideas that go against God's plan? I heard talk in the kitchen the other day that your papa has decided to marry you off to Sidney or the McDonald boy that lives on that big plantation down the river."

"Well, I'll just tell them both 'no' and hope that Papa will listen to me. Besides, maybe it'll be you jumping the broom with that new carriage man who took us to town the other day."

Early unsuccessfully tried to hold back the heat that flowed into her cheeks, before muttering, "*Non*, that will never happen."

Missy laughed and wiggled her eyebrows. "*On ne sait jamais.*"

Early's only answer was to shake her head as she kept her thoughts to herself. Missy's sentiment about not knowing what might happen could never come to be. She reached over to straighten the lacy doily that covered the marble-topped tea stand. Though she might be naive on some things, she had learned enough in the last few days to know it was best not to tell Missy that the carriage driver's dreams did not include her. His eyes focused on a real life Moses and an imagined train that would take him to Canaan Land in the far north. Nothing but trouble would come from liking him.

George

George hummed *Wade in the Water* as he rubbed oil into the leather harnesses and thought back on the eventful trip to town. That poor girl sure was clueless when it came to knowing how to act in public. Her young mistress had spoiled her. One of these days she would get herself into some real trouble if somebody didn't teach her the ways of the world. Of course, maybe she wouldn't have to worry about being obedient if she went up North with him.

Whoa there, what was he possibly thinking? A delicate filly like her would never make the trip through the Underground Railroad, with its night walks and hiding in strange places. From what he'd heard there were many folks who never made it to the North for one reason or another. Between the slave catchers and the night critters, the road to the Promised Land was supposed to be very rough. If they didn't make it, at least they would be free one way or another — whether in the arms of death or in the far lands of a place called Canada. His tune shifted to another melody about freedom. Just singing about following that drinking gourd to the North brought a smile to George's face. Then he thought again about the pampered servant girl and he puffed out a sound through his lips. A horse answered with a similar snort.

Visions of warm hazel eyes and dark curling hair drew his thoughts away from freedom and stirred another feeling deep within his chest. Granted, he had been interested in a few girls, but the thought of giving his heart to anyone never crossed his mind before. Horses and carriages, but never marriage... Did he even have a right to choose someone for himself? Hanging the leather straps more firmly than he should have, George turned to the stalls and began to fill feedbags and rub his hand down warm noses throughout the stable. Tugging the forelock of his favorite mare, he couldn't help but compare the long lashes of both the friendly horse and the petite woman who had hidden behind her fringed lids as they traveled back from town the other day.

A banging barn door shattered his thoughts. He heard the sharp words of the master's stepson piercing the solitude of the stable. Quiet shuffling hooves gave way to prancing, pawing, and nervous whinnies as the horses reacted to the boisterous young master. His strident voice ordered the head stable man to quickly saddle a favorite mount for another ride into town. A call from the headman, Old John, sent George into action.

Grabbing an ornately decorated set of tack, George moved to help prepare the white-faced mare for what would surely be another hard ride under the demanding young man's whip. As he placed a blanket over the poor horse's mid-section, he couldn't help but notice the strap marks on her rump. Shuddering as he remembered several beatings of his own, he continued to lift the saddle into place. He gave the unlucky beast a gentle poke in the side as he tightened the strap around her girth. Smelling the odor of alcohol before actually seeing Sidney let George know that things were once again going to be rough for the faithful little steed.

"Come on, man. How long can it take to saddle a horse? Maybe I need to trade your lazy hide for someone who will get the job done a little faster." Sidney glared at George and then recognition spread across his face. A scornful sneer and a low-throated snarl emanated from deep in man's chest as the groomsman led the mare from her stall.

"Well, look who we have here. If it isn't the women's little carriage driver..." The whip tapping on Sidney's left hand kept George in a position of obedience, but inside, the anything but little carriage man seethed. Praying for strength, George forced himself to relax the tense muscles flexed across his broad shoulders. He resisted using the strength in his hands. Those hands could control strong horses, lift huge loads of hay, or cut a man like Sidney down to size.

"You just stick to doing your job, you hear me, boy? I've got some special plans for that woman and I don't need her sullied by the likes of you."

George reacted with a tightened fist to both the sting of Sidney's words and the whip's lash, which burned like a branding iron across his upper arm.

A strong hand grasped George's other shoulder and spoke quietly to the brash young master. "Begging your pardon, sir, but I've got work this man needs to be doing back in the stalls."

"Make sure he earns his keep and don't let him go off to the kitchen to beg for any sweets today." Sidney tapped the whip on his side as several horses snorted and whinnied.

"No sir. We got plenty to keep us busy. Come on, son, you got some stalls to clean." John shoved a pitchfork into George's hands.

Nodding, George moved out of the irritating man's sights and began to take out his fury on the manure-filled stall recently vacated by the hapless mare. The poor beast now raced down the road at a lightning speed. His arm ached from the whip's lash but it only fueled his anger, making him work harder. Old John cleared his throat as he raised his questioning eyes toward George's irate countenance.

"Better watch your step, George. That's one mean fellow who's gaining more power around here every time he struts into this ole barn."

"Maybe someday I won't have to worry about him anymore. I'll find me a train headed north one of these spring evenings." He reached in his pocket and felt the lump he'd stitched in place. The man from Ohio had given him something called a compass that would point him in the right direction. George's stitching would hold it in place until he needed directions. "When the right time comes, I'll follow that old gourd up in the night sky 'til I don't have to see this place ever again."

"What about the girl? Who's he talking about that's got you so wound up?"

"It's Missy's girl. She thinks her mistress will take care of her, so what do I care? Not much I can do about it anyway if I'm going to get out of here. She's just some girl I've only seen a time or two."

"Hmmm... Just some girl that's got you so tied up in knots that you're cleaning up this stall like the devil is after you." John smirked and raised his eyebrows.

"Maybe the serpent himself is after me. Didn't you see him riding out of here a few minutes ago?" George swiped his shirt sleeve across his forehead and leaned on the pitchfork.

"Sure enough, son, sure enough..."

Both men shared a laugh as they envisioned the young rascal racing down the road in his red coat and white plumed hat. Their mirth tempered off as they later spoke of pity for the poor piece of horseflesh. The mare probably sported a full coat of lather by now as she tore down the road, carrying her rider to his destination. It would be a destination filled with whiskey and brimming with sin.

Returning to their chores, the two worked in companionable silence as they moved straw into cleaned stalls and filled mangers with fresh hay and grain. They'd turned the horses out into corrals and pastures for exercise. The day's routine moved on uneventfully until a piercing scream rang out from the laundry house, located at the back of the main house's kitchen.

"Snake," someone cried. A second shout sounded more than an octave higher than the initial cry.

Grabbing a hoe that leaned against the weather-beaten cedar wall of the horse barn, George ran toward the sound as John loped along behind him, toting a rake from the stack of hay they had worked on.

"Help!" This time the voice was smaller and shaky, as fear seemed to invade the familiar voice coming from inside the laundry.

Cautiously, George peered into the dim space and spotted Early huddled in the far corner of the moisture-filled room. "Where is it Early?"

"Over by the fireplace, I think it's trying to skin itself, but it doesn't look like it wants to move. I'm not moving either until it's gone."

With raised hoe in hand, George crept toward the fireplace, hoping against hope that the snake was too tired from shedding its skin to want to attack anyone. Spotting the slim black body, he couldn't help a chuckle from escaping as the creature flicked its tongue and appeared to be quite harmless.

"Quit your laughing and hurry up and kill the thing, George. What are you waiting for?" Early held up a dripping petticoat and hid behind it.

"It's just a black snake." George choked back another laugh.

"My point exactly. Now use your hoe and get rid of it."

"I'll take care of him." He wandered over to have a closer look at the snake.

By this time, John stood in the door and started his own snickering. George picked up the squirming reptile and turned to show Early the harmless critter. John's laughter echoed from the yard as he made his way back toward the horse barn.

"Look here, Early. It's just a little black snake that will probably grow up to keep the mice out of the barn one of these days."

"You can take it to the barn then, just don't let it ever come in here again. I don't like snakes."

"There's some snakes I don't like either, Miss Early, especially the one that I saw at the barn this morning."

"Please don't tell me you saw more snakes in the barn." She wrapped her arms around the cloth in her hand.

"No, only a human one..." Looking out the window to see that no one was checking on them, George lowered his voice to a whisper and bent close to tell Early about his encounter with Sidney. "Be careful around that man. He's more dangerous than a viper."

Chapter Four

Early

Panic rippled through Early's chest from both the warmth of his breath on the side of her face and from the quiet warning. For a moment her thoughts were no longer on the snake. Then she felt something cold brush across her hand. Snapping to attention, she backed away from the attractive man and the infernal reptile. She pointed toward the door. Their silent exchange conveyed both fear and a newfound friendship, with potential for something that she could not begin to fathom. He twisted away and took the curling snake with him. She stuffed the dripping laundry into a wicker basket and prepared to make her own exit.

Escaping the man and snake, Early scuttled out of the dim room and into sunlight. Confusion filled her mind as she thought about her warm feelings for George and her growing fear of Sidney, and snakes. Adjusting the heavier than usual load of laundry, she hefted the basket higher in her arms and hauled the soaked pile of clothes across the lawn. The water-filled clothing would require extra wringing once she reached the lines strung between several posts.

The nearby kitchen herb garden showed signs of spring growth, which would soon lend sweet scents to the lye-scented petticoats and underdrawers that weighed down Early's arms. Grabbing one of Missy's lacy chemises, she worked out her tension by twirling the white undergarment into a tight rope. Taking the twisted cloth between two hands and pushing it into itself produced a stream of water that doused the ground beneath the stretched rope lines. She vigorously shook the garment out and then pinned it to the line using hand-carved pegs designed to secure the clothes in place.

Welcome rays of warm sunshine brought slivers of peace and hope to Early as she lifted her heart toward the Lord and begged for protection for both her heart and body. Wandering thoughts soon turned to the man she was beginning to find very interesting, despite snakes and dreams of an unknown future up North. Maybe it would be better to just forget about men in general and dedicate herself to the familiar. Wasn't life with Missy good enough? Why did all these men, two in particular, have to come along and disrupt the good situation that the girls had always known? Why did life have to change? With a deep sigh, she turned back to the job at hand and released her frustration on each piece of clothing.

~~~~~

Later that afternoon, Early placed a heavy pressing iron back onto the trivet near the fireplace. She held the freshly pressed gown up to her shoulders and danced around the room. She stopped to stare at her reflection in the huge gilded mirror on Missy's wall. Laughing, she wondered what it would be like to attend a ball with Missy. Pulling the skirt wide, as she held the bodice with her other hand, Early curtsied and then spun around the room one more time. Heavy steps thumping down the hallway caused Early to stop her dreaming and hide behind Missy's changing screen with the dress. The master's racking cough filtered through Missy's doorway as he began a conversation with another man: a man that Early had come to fear.

"Here, Papa Hollings, take my handkerchief. I know you were thinking of riding out into the fields today, sir, but I would be glad to tend to that chore for you. I do have a way with the workers that will ensure your crops are planted on time. I will gladly take over any duties you feel I can handle."

Early hoped Master Hollings would not fall for the conniving voice that sprang from the sober lips of her adversary. She couldn't help but compare him to the coldblooded snake that had been crawling around the laundry. Could it be true that Sidney might someday take over the plantation? Surely, that would never happen since Missy would be the heir. She crushed the dress to her chest as she wondered what the field workers would endure under the cruel hand of the two-faced young man.

"Thank you, Sidney. I just haven't been myself lately. I'm proud of the way you've adjusted to living here. I feel like you are turning into the son I never had." More coughing ensued as the two men continued down the hall, discussing the planting season.

Rustling skirts let Early know that Missy was returning from her French lesson with her new mother, following another outing
~~~~~

into town.

"*Bonjour, mon amie.* How was your day my friend?"

"*Occupée*, it was full of work, Missy, just like any other day. I washed your clothes and ironed them as you expected." Early's tone came out a little harsher than she meant it to, and Missy's challenging stare demanded an explanation.

"What is wrong with you? Don't you know that you have one of the choicest positions for this family? You could be doing backbreaking work out in the fields, but instead you work for me. You should know better than that."

Early could hardly believe the words spewing out of her lifelong friend's mouth. Gaping, she tried to shape a reply but could only stare in horror at someone she had once thought would never betray her. Straightening her back, she closed her mouth and bowed her shaking head. "I guess I don't know what to say anymore."

Silence reigned as Early absorbed the gravity of what had just taken place. She quietly mourned the loss of her friend as she placed clean chemises into the inlayed bureau. Trying to deal with what felt like a supreme betrayal, one that could place her into the unknown work of the fields, felt more frightening than anything she had experienced in her life thus far.

Missy shuffled hair combs around on her vanity table. She stopped her restless movement and cleared her throat. "*Mon amie*?"

Early stopped folding petticoats and turned toward her mistress. Silence filled the room.

"I'm sorry, Early. I don't know what got into me. I'm not sure what to do about my new family." Missy reached out her hand.

"I'm sorry too, Missy. It's been a long day and I've been dealing with too many snakes today." Early wrapped her arms around her mistress. Tears rolled down their cheeks.

"Oh no, what happened?" Missy held out a lacy handkerchief.

Early took the embroidered fabric and dried her tears. "First there was a snake in the laundry house. There I was trying to wring out your unmentionables when the wicked creature came slithering out of nowhere."

"I should think you jumped out of your skin when you saw the serpent."

"We both did. That snake was shedding an old skin and was

moving kind of slow. But, I'm afraid I embarrassed myself by shrieking at the top of my voice." Early settled into a cushioned chair.

"So did anyone come to your rescue?"

"Unfortunately, yes."

"What do you mean by that?" Missy's raised eyebrows demanded an answer.

"It was George, and of all the snakes that could have crawled into the laundry, it was just a harmless black snake. The man dared to laugh at me."

"Aww honey, that's too bad. I have a feeling that you might be starting to like him a little bit." Missy put a hand over her heart and smiled.

"Not after he laughed at me, besides..." Early caught her words in time so that she didn't say any more about George's dreams of freedom. "Besides, he warned me to be careful around Sidney. It sounds like Sidney said something scary concerning me when he was collecting his horse from the barn today. I think if I even show any interest in George it could cost both of us dearly."

"Don't go fretting yourself, Early. As long as I'm my father's daughter, I'm not going to let anything happen to you."

"But what if something happens to Master Hollings? He hasn't sounded the best lately with that awful cough."

"He's had coughing fits before. It's probably nothing." The worried expression on Missy's face did not match her words.

"What if it is more? What will happen to me if Sidney becomes master of this house? I don't think you'll be able to hide me in your room forever."

"Don't you worry about my awful stepbrother. I will find my own handsome man to marry. We'll move to another plantation together. I could probably even manage to take your good looking fellow with us. Just think, we could have children, they would grow up together like we did and be best friends."

Both girls blushed at the thought of children. Early took a deep breath and continued the conversation. "Is that what we are, Missy? Friends? Or am I only a slave who happens to feel like a sister to you?"

Missy paused, apparently mulling over Early's question. "Listen, I'm sorry I raised my voice earlier. You and I both know there's nothing we can do about slavery, at least for now... It is what it is, but I'm going to do my best to see that you are always treated well."

"I know, Missy, but I'm starting to wonder about what life would be like if I weren't a slave." She picked up the dress she'd been dancing with and hung it in the armoire filled with a rainbow of gowns.

"Then we could truly be best friends and you wouldn't have to worry so much. Let's get some of my gowns out to admire. You should try on one of my dresses. I think you would look mighty pretty in that blue one I wore to the dinner at Summer Hall Plantation last month."

Giving each other a sisterly hug, the two young women were soon laughing as they practiced new French phrases and explored the wardrobe full of both practical and frilly garments.

"Look at this hat, Missy. Do you think I should wear it while I clean out your chamber pot?" Early posed with a feathered creation on her head as she held her nose and pointed to the porcelain container peeking out from under the bed.

"No, I think it might look nicer while you're cleaning the ashes from the fireplace."

"Maybe you should wear it, Missy, while you help me chase that snake out of the laundry room next washing day."

Prancing around, Missy's room the two women failed to notice that they had an audience. Sidney stood shadowed near the door and watched the duo as they linked arms and did a swing followed by a swirling curtsy. They realized he was there when he cleared his throat and moved fully into the room with his arms crossed. His mocking gaze moved between Early and Missy as they broke apart.

"Keep dancing, girls. I'm rather enjoying what I'm seeing even if I can't believe what you two are doing." His leering gaze moved up and down the young women.

Early quickly moved behind Missy as fear and anger coursed through her body in flashes of heat and cold in response to Sidney's presence. Grabbing a dress that lay haphazardly across the bed, Early slipped behind the dressing screen with her head bowed and thoughts in turmoil.

"Get out of my room, Sidney," Missy said. "There are some boundaries in this house that you will not cross. My room is off limits to you. Now, remove yourself."

Early peeked around the folds of her shield and watched. Missy drew herself up as tall as her petite stature would permit and glared at her stepbrother.

"Speaking of boundaries, maybe it's time you learned where your boundaries lie when it comes to your slave. For someone who grew up in the South, you should know how to act around the help." Sidney put his hands on his hips and leered at Missy.

Early laid the ridiculous headpiece she had been wearing with the other garments behind the screen. She stepped boldly from her hiding place. Trying to show no fear, she began straightening up yards of lace, ribbons, dresses, and hats that still littered the bed and chairs. Though she feared for herself, she would not leave Missy in the room alone with that man. Averting her eyes and clamping her mouth shut became harder and harder as Sidney ranted on about the relationship she had with her mistress. Ready to move to her friend's rescue, she stopped short when a cough rang out from the doorway.

"Missy. Sidney. Is there an explanation for this? The whole household is hearing the commotion coming from this room."

"We were just having a friendly conversation, Papa Hollings." Sidney's voice moved from condemnation to consolation at lightning speed when Missy's father entered the conversation. "I couldn't help admiring how hard her maid works to keep this room clean. Perhaps she could be spared to straighten up my room, too."

Early felt her face flush in anger and fear. Surely Papa Hollings would not let this happen. As three faces turned her way, she realized that she must have gasped aloud.

Missy stepped across the room and turned to her father. "I can assure you that my maid will be needed here in my room for the rest of the day." Begging eyes pleaded for her father to understand. Missy's flashing hazel eyes met watery ones as the older gentleman slowly agreed and turned to the younger man.

"Sidney, I'm afraid I have to cede to my daughter's wishes. She has always been a delicate creature and I'm afraid that she has grown to depend upon her maid for just about everything."

Early watched Missy stiffen. Her mistress relaxed when Master Hollings gave a subtle wink, letting the girls know he was just trying to lighten the conflict that had ensued.

"Come along, Sidney. Your mother informs me that you were quite the scholar when it came to working with figures. I've been having a little trouble balancing the numbers in my record books and could sure use your assistance." Missy's father escorted Sidney from the room.

"I can't help but wonder what kind of figures he worked on at school. It was probably some hapless female figure instead of a budget tally," Missy complained to Early. They closed the door and carefully locked themselves away from any other prying eyes.

Missy

Missy watched as Early picked up the remaining clothing and scurried behind the screen to hang the gowns in the armoire. She wanted to say something to set her friend free, but that was the issue. She could not. She didn't have that right. Only Papa had that power.

Anger boiled in her cinched waist, bound tightly to conform to fashion and society norms. Those social demands placed the young woman hanging her clothes at her beck and call. It put Early in a position where she must do her mistress's bidding because she had no freedom. Was their friendship a farce? Did Early serve and provide companionship because she had to, because she was a slave? She plopped onto the edge of her high bed. Early came to her side. Her eyes were averted and uncertain. Missy tentatively laid her hand on Early's tense shoulder.

"We will always be like sisters in my mind."

Early lowered her shoulders but worry still crowded her eyes. "But can you stop Sidney from tearing us apart?"

"I don't know, but I will try."

Amanda chose that moment to enter the room. "I hope you will try to act more like a Southern young lady, instead of simpering over your slave girl. Early, go to the kitchen. Make yourself useful by helping Nellie as she prepares for our evening meal." Amanda stepped through the doorway and Early slid out to do her bidding. "Have a seat. It's time we have a little talk."

Missy sank into a chair, dreading the lecture that was sure to come. She closed her eyes as the tirade began.

"Are you listening to me, Melissa?"

Missy squirmed and forced an attentive expression across her face.

"A young lady of your standing needs to behave in a certain way. I see that your father has neglected to teach you proper etiquette for the society you should be keeping. We will start with running a household. You are the superior of any servant. They are to follow your directions without questioning. Slaves are not your friends."

Missy's mind wandered as Amanda droned on. She did rely on the household servants for most, if not all of her needs. The rest of the servants might not be as close as Early, but they'd always felt like family, until now. Her stepmother wanted to change everything. She sighed.

"Sit up, girl. You are ruining your posture. Now where was I? You need to have the skill to run your own home when you marry."

Missy began to feel a knot in her back as she stiffly sat and pretended to listen. Amanda's words sounded like nonsense to her ears, kind of like the nonsense limericks in Lear's book that still sat on a nearby bookshelf. She'd enjoyed those silly stories as a child. She could still hear the pattern of words.

> *There was a new mistress of Holly,*
> *Who blamed all the slaves for her folly.*
> *They did as she said*
> *With haste and bowed head*
> *And disliked the mistress of Holly.*

~~~~~

The next morning, Missy smiled to herself as she watched Sidney tug at the wine cabinet door. "You won't be able to open any bottles today."

Sidney turned and glared at her. His eyes roamed from her face down to her hands and back to her eyes. "Guess I'll have to get to know my stepsister a little better instead, since Papa has taken away one of my pleasures. Would you care to take a walk with me?" His glare changed to an amorous leer as he pushed closer.

"No thank you. I believe Papa has other plans for you today." Relief filled Missy when she heard her father's raspy voice talking to Moses about something in the entrance hall. She gave her
~~~~~

stepbrother a triumphant lift of her chin, then turned and made her way toward the sound. Sidney followed as she greeted her father with a hug.

Sidney interrupted their embrace with a chuckle. "Good morning, Papa Hollings. I was just enjoying a merry conversation with Missy." Sidney's voice sounded as sweet as molasses cookies.

Missy shuddered and shook her head. Papa didn't seem to notice as he patted Sidney on the back.

"That's wonderful, son. I'm happy to see that my children are starting to get along." He stood taller and paused to breathe.

"Why, thank you, sir. Perhaps we can all take a stroll and you can teach me more about how to successfully run this plantation together, as a family." The smile across his face did not match his gloating eyes.

"Excuse me, I have to practice the new embroidery stitch that Mother Amanda taught me." Missy huffed as she made a quick exit. She couldn't believe the transformation in Sidney the snake. One minute he was vile and the next he was kind to her father. If God had wanted to name the serpent in the Garden of Eden, he could have called it 'Sidney.' At least Papa had the sense to lock up the hard drinks, for now. Not that it mattered much; Sidney had a way of finding trouble on his own.

Chapter Five

Early

Early breathed in the welcome smell of spring. The scent of sun-dried laundry filled the air as she changed Missy's bed linens. Sidney's recent attentiveness to Papa Hollings brought a sense of normalcy to the plantation as things seemed to settle into a routine during the last few days. Papa Hollings continued to make sure that any strong spirits remained locked up and designated for medicinal purposes only. The two young women kept to themselves in the confines of Missy's room. Sometimes they hid in childhood haunts known only to them, from days when they were small. Sidney didn't know everything about the plantation and they kept the best secrets hidden from his prying eyes.

Early sprinkled crushed lavender between the sheets and lifted her fingers to her nose. The relaxing scent made her want to lift her hands in praise to the Lord. Earlier in the day, she enjoyed picking the herb in the kitchen garden. The hearty plant had managed to survive the cooler weather of the past winter. Not only had she found the early blooming lavender, she'd also enjoyed a glimpse of the horse barn where a certain carriage driver happened to parade a handsome horse around the yard. She'd admired the man's flexing muscles as he hung out saddle blankets in the fresh air. Her thoughts returned to smoothing out Missy's covers and plumping her pillows.

Missy sat nearby with her head bent over writing paper. Her pen scratched across a page and then fell silent. She sighed and wadded the paper up before tossing it into the fireplace. "Early, please make sure these papers are burned. I'm not finding the words I need to say right now and I don't want anyone finding my poorly attempted rhymes."

"It's a little warm today. I can wait until later if that's all right."

"No. Please do it now. I cannot risk your safety or mine."

Early picked up the tinder box, checked the fireplace's flue, and leaned over the papers that had accumulated on the grate. Words about slavery's curse caught her eye. What was Missy up to? Flames consumed the words as she backed away and turned to her mistress. She threw her last bit of lavender into the fire, hoping it would soothe Missy's worries. "Do you need help?"

"I guess maybe I do. What is it like to be a slave? Is it so bad?"

Early looked at the floor and then back at her mistress. She lifted her chin and asked, "Do you really want to know, even if it hurts?"

Missy nodded and swiped away a tear that coursed down her cheek. "Help me understand. I want to try to right a wrong. I need to put your voice into my poetry."

Interlude-Ginny

Ginny flipped through a couple of pages in the journal and the loose papers. She ran her fingers over a few jagged edges where it looked like paper had been ripped from the journal. She couldn't find poetry from another hand or voice that would reflect Early's thoughts. Disappointment welled up in her chest. She felt like a hound dog denied a favorite treat. Jezebel pawed her owner's leg and looked up with begging eyes. Had she said 'treat' out loud or did her mutt read minds? Stretching, she stood and got the dog a bone. She grabbed an ice cream sandwich from the freezer for herself. The dim glow of an orange-tinted harvest moon filled the fall sky. Her mind was getting too foggy to continue taking notes from Missy's words.

Maybe a change in perspective would be good. She could grade papers or investigate some of the library books she'd picked up after school. Flipping through her bag of tomes, her focus fell upon an older book she'd located in the library book sale room called *To Be a Slave*. It proclaimed itself as a collection of actual accounts from those who had once been in slavery.

Woman and dog snuggled on the couch for a cozy reading time. The book pulled the reader back in time. She'd been a little amazed by the friendship between the two women proclaimed in Missy's journal. However, as she read through the accounts, there were several stories about people who worked as house slaves becoming like family to their owners. Those who served in the fields often disliked their counterparts in the plantation house.

Field workers endured harsh treatment from long work hours and beatings, while some house servants were treated much better. An interesting idea floated across her thoughts: could George have some disregard for the privileged Early? Stories like the ones Ginny had read in the journal were rare, though. Most of the stories in *To Be a Slave* relayed unhappiness, cruelty, and a longing to be free. George's desire to escape seemed to be more the norm. Maybe Missy didn't record Early's thoughts because they were too harsh or not troublesome enough for consideration in the abolitionist paper.

Leaving a snoozing Jezebel on the couch, Ginny returned to the table and opened the next letter sticking out of the journal. The return address was Winston County, Alabama. She'd seen the area mentioned in an earlier letter. Curious, she tapped the location into her phone's search engine and was amazed as a photo of an historical marker popped up. Winston County, once known as Hancock County, had refused to leave the Union during the Civil War. The hilly area had not been good for plantation crops, so very few people held anyone in slavery. They became the Free State of Winston two years before the Civil War began. Very interesting...

Winston County
Alabama

Dearest Brother Arthur,

This letter is to inform you that I will be arriving near the end of the month. I will send a detailed telegram once I purchase my train tickets. I have decided to leave my life as a hill country farm wife now that Frederick has gone to his reward. Our Ohio sister, Mary Etta, has room for me at Woodson House and that is where I plan to stay after I reacquaint myself with your daughter. Which brings me to one of the purposes of my visit: I would like to take your Melissa on a trip, with your permission of course. Perhaps she and her servant girl can be my traveling companions as I see the southern countryside one last time before retiring to the north. That being said, with the sale of the farm, I would like to purchase at least one of your gentled mares and a sturdy conveyance for my travels. I always admired the good horse stock, which you and our parents before us raised at Holly

Plantation.

There are some other private matters that we must discuss but I will hold those back until we meet in person. I hope you are maintaining your health, dear brother. Mary Etta's nephew mentioned that you were coughing at your wedding and still reeked of tobacco. Hopefully your new bride will convince you to give up that nasty habit.

Your Concerned Sister,
Miranda Hollings McCallum

Early

Early picked up the discarded letter Master Hollings had dropped in the trash bin in his office. More and more the new mistress had forced her to clean other rooms, taking her away from Missy. Some days, the separation from Missy filled her with frustration and the fear of Sidney finding her alone. Other days, it gave her access to information, like the letter she held in her hand. She slipped from the room and made her way up the stairs to where Missy stood gazing out a lace-covered window.

"You might want to look at Aunt Matilda's letter. It sounds like there's more to her visit than we've been told."

Missy flattened the letter on a table and studied it. "I wonder what private matter she has with Papa?" Her brow creased as she folded the letter and tucked it into her journal. "I'm glad she still wants to take us on a journey. We can both use some time away from Sidney."

Early nodded in agreement. She stepped away when they heard a cleared throat from the doorway. The new mistress stood with her arms crossed, a frown marred her face. "If you have finished dusting the master's office, then I need you to start polishing the silver. We just received a telegram from Melissa's Aunt Matilda. She will be here on Friday."

~~~~~

When the day came to retrieve Aunt 'Tilda from the train station, Missy insisted Early attend her so she would be presentable for the occasion. Both Amanda and Sidney chose to wait at home. Moses assisted Early onto the high carriage seat before finding his
~~~~~

way to sit in the boot. Her heart fluttered as she settled next to the driver.

"Good morning, George."

"If you say so." George turned his attention to the horses. He jostled the reins and clicked his tongue.

Early grabbed the edge of the wooden bench when the carriage jerked forward. "What is the matter with you?"

"Nothing I can do anything about." He sat silently for several moments before speaking again. "Missy's Aunt Matilda is looking for a horse and it sounds like the master is going to sell my favorite mare as part of the bargain."

"I'm sorry, but she's just a horse. It isn't like you are losing your best friend." Early's thoughts wandered to her changing relationship with Missy.

George's muttered reply interrupted her thoughts. "You wouldn't understand. You've never been sold from your home before, or should I say yet."

Early's blood ran cold as the possibility of being sold away from Missy blistered its way through her veins. "I have no idea what it would be like, but I do live in fear of keeping my position, with the new mistress in charge."

They rode without speaking until they reached the small depot where Aunt Matilda's train would arrive. George sat stoically on his high perch as Moses helped Early climb down to assist her mistress. She brushed Missy's skirts and adjusted the feathered hat so it sat at a perky angle. Then she took her place a few steps back from the master and his daughter.

Shock tumbled through her body as the metal monstrosity rumbled down the tracks and then hissed to a stop in a cloud of burning ashes. Such a wicked sounding beast! Even the ground shook in fear. She hoped George's railway to the north would not be making steam and cinders fly through the air as it puffed him away to freedom. He'd surely be caught if it did. A uniformed man swung down from the train and positioned steps in front of an open doorway.

A woman dressed in a simple calico frock stepped onto the platform and waved toward Master Hollings. This must be Missy's aunt. Years ago, Early had hidden away with her mother in a tiny room near the basement fireplace during Aunt Matilda's last visit.

She had no idea why they hid other than following the master's orders. She'd enjoyed being the center of her mother's attention for a week. They both welcomed the sunshine and Missy's warm hugs, when the visit ended. Now, when she wished she could vanish, she stood in attendance, waiting to meet Aunt Matilda.

She gaped in surprise as Missy's Aunt 'Tilda bustled down from the steps of the puffing train. The woman shook her dress in disdain as bits of cinders and crumbs from what must have been a late lunch fell to the ground in a cloud of dust. A yipping dog dared to step in front of her as he searched for an errant crumb. The powerful woman ordered it from her path. She gave the pup a firm push with her walking stick and spoke warning words for the beast to get out of her way. When the dog obeyed and sat quietly, she pulled a piece of bread from her reticule and tossed it toward the animal.

Early couldn't help but wonder what it would be like to be so daring. Just knowing that such a woman existed made her stand a little taller as she waited near Missy for the aunt to make her way in their direction. Early had been in awe of the hissing train but she was even more amazed by the woman who now stepped toward the two waiting members of the Hollings family.

"I see you're still holding to the slave tradition, brother. You really must read some of the books I've got tucked away in my trunk. A little literature from the North might prove enlightening."

"Now Matilda, you know it's the way of life down here." Master Hollings ground out the comment in a way that begged for discretion, as people turned with questioning eyes. Early and Missy moved into the shadow of the coach in an effort to avoid the frowning faces.

"My, my, brother. What have you done to your voice? It sounds like too much tobacco smoke, if you ask me. Someday people are going to realize what a hazard smoking is to your health. I hope that some of this good warm air will solve your problem. Now, who are these lovely young women? Surely I can't be looking at little Melissa, all grown up?"

Clearing his throat, Papa turned to his daughter and confirmed that she truly was his grown offspring.

"And this other young lady?"

His simple introduction of Early as Missy's house servant

raised the aunt's eyebrows as she 'tsk-tsked' and swiveled her focus between the two young women's eyes.

"Her maid certainly has interesting eyes, brother, very interesting indeed."

Master Hollings coughed and rocked from one foot to the other. "I, uh, hope you had a pleasant trip, Matilda."

"It was tolerable but I've learned to make do on my own. Since my husband passed and before, I handled my affairs without ever needing the help of slave labor. You might be surprised how liberating that can be, Arthur." Aunt 'Tilda slipped her arm through her brother's as she pulled him in the direction of a small steamer trunk.

Early stared into Missy's face and for a moment it was like looking into her own hazel eyes and dimpled cheeks. It had always been a mysterious thing that the two bore similar eyes. In the past they enjoyed making a game out of pretending to be real sisters. Though their relationship had been sheltered, both knew that some questions were best left unanswered.

Papa's ragged voice ended their reverie as he called on George and Moses to carry the trunk and a colorful carpet bag to the family's crested coach. After tucking the baggage into the boot of the large conveyance, the two men servants assisted the family into the carriage and Early once again found herself being hoisted up to the high bench. Though the enclosed family carriage boasted a longer driver's bench, Early found herself pressed even closer to George when Moses pushed in beside her. There was no longer room for the older man in the boot due to Aunt Matilda's steamer trunk. Suddenly breathing became an issue as she found herself leaning against the whole side of the muscular carriage driver. Warm breath brushed her cheek. He turned and looked at her with a question reflected from his handsome face.

"The heat's not causing you to lose your breath, is it, Miss Early?"

Shaking her head to answer negatively, Early forced air into her lungs and sat straighter, hoping to give herself a little space. Unfortunately, just as she managed to make a small gap, the horses turned sharply and George slid even closer to Early on the bench. His grin and Moses' knowing chuckle were all Early needed to rein in her thoughts about the man. Staring straight ahead, she shook her head in disgust and muttered something about men under her breath.

"Did you say something, Early?" He looked her way with raised brows.

Her tight lips trembled in both reaction to the handsome man and embarrassment as she stared at his much too perfect face. "Nothing you would want to know. By the way, you can call me Miss Early."

"Did Miss Early say you could come a'calling on her?" Moses couldn't help but put in his teasing comment.

"I'm not sure, Moses, but I might be more interested if Miss Early wasn't so uppity."

Early couldn't help but notice the emphasis put on her title and decided that perhaps a little levity might draw attention away from the situation.

"At least I got an introduction to the visitor. I didn't see that happening for you two mule-headed men, unless you count: Go get that trunk and let's get going, boys." Wagging her fingers at the two, she struck a pose of being in charge and couldn't resist poking her elbows into the two men, who jumped apart, giving her more room, allowing her breathing a chance to return to normal.

In the silence that followed, laughter echoed from inside the carriage as Missy and Aunt 'Tilda conversed with Master Hollings. Early relaxed and began asking George questions about the matched team of horses that pranced ahead of them. She hoped the men would forget their teasing and entertain her with stories of the regal steeds that pulled the carriage down the dusty road leading out of town.

Missy

As Missy and Aunt Matilda stepped from the carriage, Sidney greeted them, providing an assisting elbow. His syrup-filled voice welcomed Aunt Matilda to the plantation as he assisted her from the carriage with a greeting. "Welcome, my lady, to our home."

"I know all about Holly Plantation, young man. I grew up here. This was my home until I came to my senses and married my farmer, Frederick.

If Aunt's comment affected Sidney, he didn't show it. Instead he reached for Missy's elbow and held it closely to his side, despite her resistance after her feet landed on firm ground. She tried to push him away, but he tightened his grip.

He simpered. "Welcome back, honey. I can see where you get your charm."

Disgust slithered across her hand when he turned and kissed her fingers. She jerked her arm away and backed into Papa as he climbed down the steps.

"Are you all right, Missy?" Papa sounded winded after he caught his balance.

"Sorry, Papa, I thought I saw a snake." Missy glared at her stepbrother.

Aunt Matilda chuckled. "I definitely think there is a snake in the grass, and his name is Sidney."

Papa looked confused. Aunt Matilda laughed and motioned for Missy to come to her side.

"If you men will see to my belongings, I'd like to take a little stroll around the place with Melissa." She linked arms with her niece and headed toward a bench under one of the live oaks standing like sentinels surrounding the plantation home. As they sat down, she pointed up to the cupola at the top of the house. "I used to hide out in the cupola when I was your age and my pa punished a slave. I didn't like it. I still don't like slavery. Sometimes I even felt like a slave because I had to do what Pa told me to do."

"I know that feeling well, Aunt 'Tilda."

"Then tell me about it, child." The older woman sandwiched Missy's right palm between her own calloused hands.

"I'm so scared at times. I'm afraid that Papa will force me to marry Sidney or some other plantation owner. If that happens, what will happen to Early? When she opened the windows in that cupola a while back, Sidney came after her to—well, I don't want to think about what he might have done if she hadn't come into my room and locked the door. Sidney brags about making the slaves behave. I know he carries a whip and a cruel attitude. I don't want to stay here and be a slave owner. I don't want Sidney to have power over me or anyone that I love."

"Do you love Early?"

"I love her better than any sister I might have had."

"What about the other slaves?"

"I don't know them as well, but I'm willing to do something to tell anyone who will listen about the curse of slavery."

"Really? How do you plan to do that?"

"I have written some poetry, much of it with Early's help. Aunt Mary Etta's nephew promised to share it in a newspaper if I can get it to him. In fact, I have some pieces that I'd like you to send to him through Aunt Mary Etta when you post another letter to her."

"Excellent, my dear young woman. Now tell me more about Mary Etta's nephew. I've never met the young man in person."

Chapter Six

Early

As Early aired out the adjoining room to Missy's for Aunt 'Tilda, she hummed a sweet spiritual she had learned from her mother. Her beloved parent had experienced no fear when she had to cross over Jordan. She didn't have to cross alone because she loved the Lord Jesus and made sure that Early and Missy knew all about Him. *I may be a dying but it's just to this old earth. You two darling girls better let Jesus know you're His so I can see you over there in heaven.* Early smiled at the memories as she pulled back the covers for Aunt 'Tilda's feather bed and hummed another verse of the comforting song.

"Well, that's a mighty pretty tune, woman. Maybe you should sing more often."

Dread shook Early as she looked toward the door and saw a sober Sidney watching her every movement from across the room. She averted her eyes and looked around the bedroom for something to use for protection. Her thoughts proved unnecessary, as Aunt 'Tilda swept into the room in a cloud of lavender scent. Barging past the startled young man, she placed both hands on his shoulders and pushed him from the room with a huff. Snapping the door closed, she grinned at Early's gaping mouth.

"If I'm not mistaken, that young scallywag needs to learn some manners. Now, young lady, let me help you puff up these pillows a little bit."

"But ma'am, it's my job to refresh your room."

"Stuff and bother, Early. It may be your job but there's no law that says I can't help out some with a few chores, is there?"

"Maybe not where you're from, ma'am, but I'm not sure about around here anymore—that is unless you're someone special like Missy is to me." Early almost hesitated to speak so boldly to the older woman, but seeing how she commanded openness from others, she couldn't resist the opportunity to talk freely with the matron, who already pushed around the feathers in an overstuffed pillow.

"So tell me about this special relationship you have with my niece."

"We're almost like sisters—that is, except for the color of our skin. Most days we don't even stop to think about it, but lately I've been noticing...." Early's thoughts drifted off as she cast a quick look at the observant woman and wondered if she had said too much.

"It's all right, lass. I won't tell anyone your thoughts. I'm very much opposed to slavery and there are many people up north, and here in the South, who think just like me. Slavery never took hold in the hill country where my husband and I lived. I was happy to leave plantation life behind when I married my Frederick. Now look at me up close. I want to see those eyes of yours gazing proudly at the world." Aunt 'Tilda's own hazel eyes seemed to probe the very depths of Early's soul as she held the younger woman's chin. The aunt appeared to be searching for a missing clue to something. Discomfort filled Early as she shifted her gaze to the floor.

Awkwardly, Early slipped away from 'Tilda's hands and grabbed another pillow to fluff.

"So tell me about your mother, Early."

"She was a good woman. She raised Missy and me together here in this very room. It used to be the nursery and Mama filled it with enough love for both of us to share."

"Do you remember anything about Missy's mother?"

"Not really. I don't recall exactly what happened to Missy's real mother, but the story coming from one of my friends in the kitchen said she might have died of a broken heart. All I know is that for as long as I can remember it was just the three of us, like a cozy little family."

"Did you ever know your daddy?"

"No, Mama never talked about him. She only wanted me to know my Heavenly Father so I could go to the good place someday. I always wondered about my earthly father, though. I would have liked my papa to have been as nice as Papa Hollings has been to Missy."

'Tilda harrumphed instead of adding to the conversation. A perplexed expression crossed her face as she took another look at Early. "At least you seem to have escaped the worst ravages of slavery through some kind of Fatherly providence."

"I pray to my heavenly Father every day, ma'am." Early smoothed the bed covering and stepped away. "Is there anything else you need?"

"Yes dear, I should like some writing materials. I need to answer some correspondence."

Early opened the doors to the small secretary where Missy secretly taught her to write, when the room housed the nursery. She folded down the desk table, revealing a collection of papers, feathered quills, and blackberry ink in a corked bottle. Seeing no evidence of her own or Missy's writing efforts, she sighed in relief and waved Aunt Matilda toward the writing implements.

"Would you like anything else, ma'am?"

"Yes, you will refer to me as Aunt Matilda when we are in this room."

"Thank you, ma'am, I mean Aunt 'Tilda, uh, Matilda." Early giggled and made her way to the door.

"And Early, if that young man wandering the halls bothers you again, let me know."

Holly Plantation
April 1858

Dear Mary Etta,

The matter of the girls is indeed pressing. The family resemblance is remarkable and undeniable evidence that we do have two nieces. They must have hidden the other girl away when I saw Melissa as a child. I hope Arthur has enough sense left in him to let us carry out a plan. I dare say before this year is over, we will need to make use of your guest rooms at Woodson House, including the hidden one that reminds me of our childhood adventures here at the plantation's dragon den. You were smart to include that memorable place in your reconstruction of our old home.

Both of our nieces have matured into beautiful women, from their hazel eyes down to the dimples in their cheeks. Their Hollings' heritage is strong and I fear that the new stepson has designs toward both young women. If we do not rescue them from the situation sometime this summer I fear for their purity.

So far they have been sheltered from the storms of this world but that will soon change one way or the other.

I am looking forward to joining your family in the near future. I already sent two trunks your way for safe keeping. All of my other belongings are a gift for the farm's new owner. I sold my Winston County, Alabama land to a good free man and his family. I pray they will see many harvests but the land isn't as productive as Arthur's here in plantation country. The Winston County neighbors have taken a stand against the slavery that surrounds less hilly counties. Should rumors of a war over slavery ever come to fruition, I fear for the safety of my former neighbors who would surely side with the North.

Our niece Melissa has a talent for poetry and she has developed a dislike for slavery, a curse that keeps her in buttons and bows. It seems that your husband's nephew made quite the appeal for the abolition movement while he visited her at the wedding. Her eyes seem to hold a certain sparkle when she speaks of the young man. I hope he is worthy of her gentle spirit. She has drawn enough courage to write several poems that he might be able to use in his efforts. I am enclosing some of her verses with my letter. She lives in fear that her words may be intercepted if she attempts to communicate on her own. I see that her fears may indeed be rooted in reality as I observe Amanda and Sidney.

Please offer daily prayers for me as I deal with Arthur and his new family. I must say I have enjoyed meeting with the youngest members of the Hollings family tree, our sweet nieces.

Your loving sister,
Matilda Hollings McCallum

Forest Glen, Ohio
Samuel

Samuel shifted on his feet as the woman in front of him read most of her letter aloud. Having the post office in his print shop often proved interesting when customers shared their news. Most epistles didn't affect him personally. His Aunt Mary Etta frequently shared any family news with him, but this time her letter concerned the young woman whose image kept appearing in his daydreams.

He had pushed her visage out of his thoughts many times since his return to Forest Glen.

The southern belle should mean nothing to him. She stood in total opposition to all that he believed in. She would never measure up to his Rebecca, who had worked hard to provide a warm home for their little family. Too bad his sweetheart had died in childbirth a year after their young marriage had begun. He had no plans for marrying again, especially to a helpless plantation girl. She probably didn't have enough sense to realize that the maid who did all her work was clearly her own flesh and blood. Would she even care if she knew? There was enough heartache in the world. His thoughts shouldn't even connect spoiled Missy Hollings with marriage. He could use the excuse that she was a cousin but Aunt Mary Etta had made it clear that the two shared no blood lines. She'd even winked and declared his uncle had survived quite well married to a Southern gal. Regardless, the call to serve others, through his newspaper and by traveling the South with information for those who wanted freedom, filled his life.

"Are you listening? Samuel?" Mary Etta pushed papers against his chest. A whiff of lavender emanated from the sheets along with a hint of inky berries. The curly penmanship further identified the writer as female, the shape of the worded forms poetic. So, she had actually risen to his challenge. He sank against his desk, set the personal letter aside and browsed the poetry. The message in the poems touched his hardened soul. He closed his eyes, looked heavenward, and prayed for strength to resist the woman while using her poems for good.

Early

Early glanced up at the sky and couldn't resist filling her lungs with the night air as she took in the blanket of stars dotting God's dark blue heavens. A half moon partially lit the sky as sparkling patterns of stars wove a tapestry across the dark expanse. Could that big gourd in the heavens truly be a map to freedom or was it just a fairy tale like the ones she had heard when Missy's tutors were trying to teach the young mistress how to read?

The life she knew with Missy had begun to feel more and more like a work of fiction since Sidney had entered their little world.

Over the course of the spring season she'd come to believe men could be both dangerous and confusing. Shaking her head at her wandering thoughts, she quickly stepped into the servants' necessary and took care of her business before beginning her trek toward the back entrance to the basement room where she should be sleeping. Amanda recently discovered her sleeping arrangements with Missy and had sent her back to the cellar. Nellie now slept on the outside of their bed while Early slept against the wall. The older woman's snores had awakened Early's urge to visit the outhouse. Too bad they didn't have a chamber pot like the one in Missy's room.

Distracted by a lightning bug, Early almost missed a shadow that passed by the side of the house. However, there was no missing the twanging voice as Sidney sang an off-tune sonnet. His shadow faded into the reality of the man behind the singing. Fearing discovery, Early stepped between the barn and a shed. Strong, warm arms pulled her further into the darkness, no longer lit by the moon. She stiffened in fear.

George

"It's all right, Early. I won't let him find you, so don't you dare scream." George felt the tense woman begin to relax in his arms so he loosed his hold. He instantly missed her warmth but knew it was a wiser choice to release her. He stepped back and motioned for her to follow him further between the buildings. Reaching for her hand seemed the right thing to do as he led the way to the far side of the buildings. He second-guessed his action, as a warm tingle seemed to stretch through their connection. Dropping her hand almost as fast as he had taken it, he paused to listen to the commotion occurring at the back entrance to the house.

"It's about time somebody let me in. I was out admiring the sights and couldn't seem to find what I was looking for." The crash of a wash pan falling off the back steps was followed by Moses' quiet voice as he encouraged the young master to make his way to bed.

Early's chattering teeth filled the air and touched something buried deep within George's heart. He closed the gap between them that he had so recently opened. Pulling her shaking body close to his brought him a sense of homecoming, and with a sigh, he leaned closer and tucked her head under his chin. Early's wavering seemed to increase, so he reached under her chin and gently brought her face up toward his own.

"Maybe you should come with me to freedom."

Tear-filled eyes met his as their faces grew closer and closer. "I'm scared, George."

"Me too, Early." Afraid to share a kiss, afraid of the dangerous young man, afraid to leave this woman or take her with him on a dangerous trip to freedom… His lips almost brushed hers as a hiss sounded from a shadowed figure on the walkway to the necessary. Early's head turned to the side. Loss, fear, and relief swirled deep within George's chest.

"Psssst. Early, is that you back there between the sheds? It's safe now." Missy's sharp whisper caused the couple to step further apart. Instead of a warm kiss, he laid a warning finger upon Early's lips before he faded away into the darkness. Her eyes looked in his direction before she stepped toward her mistress and grabbed her hand. The two young women, in silent accord, hurried back toward the shadowed mansion. Missy would take care of her for now. But, for how long?

George watched the twosome emerge into the light streaming from a lantern Missy's aunt held high from where she stood on the back stoop. His heartbeat began to return to normal. What had he been thinking? He couldn't get involved with the pampered young miss who didn't know her place in this harsh world. All too soon, something was going to happen to her—something he couldn't control. Reality would rear its angry head and throw her to the ground. When he left, the stampede of slavery would trample her to the ground. He wouldn't be able to save her. It was probably better that he left, rather than be here to see what evils lay ahead for the innocent woman.

Spring became more evident every day and whispered talk about the possible return of a Moses or railroad to freedom grew with intensity among the people who lived down in the quarters where he and Old John slept. It was only by the grace of God that he had wandered out of the building tonight and happened upon Early fleeing from the peril of the drunken young man.

He had stepped out under the starlit sky to see if the Ohio

man's compass really did point to the north. He fingered the treasure in his pocket and held it out in the moonlight to see if its pointer worked. The arrow spun and then pointed toward the North Star. Satisfied with the direction it gave, he dropped it back into its hidden pocket. He would stitch it back into place before going to sleep, if he didn't hear the call to leave tonight.

His trek into the dark to take in the beloved dipper and the star that pointed to the north had led to Early's safety. Perhaps God watched out for her after all. The Lord had not come to his rescue when his former master tore his family apart. Perhaps God only cared for this woman out of some twist of luck, but not for the likes of a barn slave. It seemed like household slaves had better luck than the rest of them.

Staring up into the vast, clear sky, George couldn't help but be amazed at the expanse that he had once acknowledged as God's handiwork. Deep down in his soul, he knew God existed. He just resented a Heavenly Father who took away his earthly parents. He knew he should be praying about the confusing woman and her safety. He struggled to leave her in the Lord's hands as he prepared to escape to freedom. He searched the sky for answers. Though nothing appeared except the brightly twinkling stars, a peace filled his whole being as the spring night returned to normal with quiet cricket chirps and a distant hoot of a barn owl. George listened as the owl called again, sounding almost human. Instead of going to check the source of the sound, he turned toward the house and then made his way to bed.

Chapter Seven

Early

Early carried the tray holding a platter of fried chicken and a tureen filled with pork flavored turnip greens into the formal dining room and began to carefully set the dishes in place. Master Hollings' blessing for the food had finished moments earlier. Moses stepped into the room and began to fill glasses with a red wine. She noticed Missy and Aunt Matilda declined the liquor in favor of clear water. Her mistress and her aunt had good heads on their shoulders.

Sidney leaned close and brushed against her side as she stepped around the table. He winked when she set a serving dish next to his plate. She stepped away and wiped her hands on her apron. An unclean feeling washed over her side where he had bumped into her. She wanted to go back to the kitchen and wash her hands. Nellie chose that moment to bring in the last of the food. Early knew she had no other choice but to stand close to the sideboard and assist with the rest of the meal. Aunt 'Tilda's eyes seemed to be taking in everything around the room as a frown creased her forehead.

The tinkle of silverware on china filled the next few minutes as the family began to enjoy their dinner. Early removed the serving dishes to the sideboard once the plates were filled, avoiding contact with Sidney as much as she could. Missy's mouthed apology and a pat on the hand from Aunt 'Tilda let her know they sympathized.

Sidney sipped wine from his glass. "Thank you, Papa Hollings, for allowing me to celebrate my birthday with some good spirits. I don't know why you keep the finer brews hidden. I've had to go into town for refreshment." He turned a smiling face to the master. Early fought to keep from rolling her eyes as he continued his speech. "I am so thankful that you consider me your son. I look forward to many years of pleasure as we work together for the good of Holly Plantation."

Aunt 'Tilda brought her napkin to her mouth and then lowered it as she shook her head. "From what I've heard, it seems to me that you do better when you aren't around the spirits." She glared at Sidney with an expression that rivaled Missy's strictest tutor. "Maybe you should be working on spiritual matters instead of spirits, young man."

Amanda tapped on the edge of her goblet. "A toast to my spirit-filled son on his birthday." She raised her glass and all responded except for Matilda, who harrumphed and stabbed her fork into a bite of chicken. Missy barely touched her lips to the rim, before setting her water down. Sidney drained his wineglass and lifted it for a refill.

"Fill up my glass, woman." He turned and eyed Early. Hanging her head, she stepped closer with the decanter. She hated having Sidney make her do his bidding. She hated what wine did to people. A calm resolve crept over her. She lifted the container and only filled the glass halfway. She caught a glimpse of Aunt 'Tilda's wink as she stepped back from the table. Lifting her head higher, she set the decanter on the sideboard and resumed her position beside it.

Sidney smirked as his hand swept across the table. His half-filled goblet tipped and rolled over, onto the white table covering. Dark color spread like a bleeding wound. "Oh my, what a mess I seem to have made. The wine is sure to permanently stain the cloth if not cleaned immediately, don't you think, Mother?"

"As usual you are right, son. Woman, see that this is cleaned now." She shook out her napkin and dropped it on top of the spreading puddle.

Master Hollings stood. "Perhaps we should have our dessert in the library." He nodded to the group and led them from the table.

Sidney laughed. "I may wait to have my dessert until later."

Early grimaced and stepped closer to remove plates, silver, and glasses from the table. Moses handed her a cleaning cloth from the kitchen and she wrapped it around the blood red stain. Nellie stepped from the kitchen with a basket. Early pushed the sopping wet table covering into the basket and headed into the twilight. The darkened laundry building loomed ahead. Its door creaked as she stepped inside.

The smell of lye soap filled the room as she blindly felt her way to the tub where she scrubbed the family laundry. Pushing the tablecloth into the iron container, she ran her fingers along the mantle for the flint she'd use to strike the wood and kindling she had laid out a few days before. A chill ran up her spine as she remembered the snake George removed. Hopefully the vile animal stayed in the barn where George thought it belonged. *Tap, tap...* Early jumped. The sounds of footsteps in the room were not from a snake. A dark figure drew nearer.

"Moses? Did you bring water?"

"No, woman. It's time you learned who your real master is," Sidney's hand over her mouth stifled Early's scream.

Struggling to get away, she pushed hard into his chest. He stumbled backwards and the iron cauldron filled with the soiled laundry toppled from its stand and rolled across the floor, clanging and banging.

Sidney cursed and snarled. "My foot. You'll pay for this one day, woman."

Early fled from the room and hid behind bushes. She watched as Moses entered the laundry building carrying a pail of water. Moments later he guided the hobbling man to the plantation house. Howls of pain filled the air and were then quieted somewhere deep in the mansion. She cautiously reentered the laundry, set the kettle back upright, and poured the bucket of water over the tablecloth to soak. She didn't need any further wrath from the missus over the stained cover.

Once that chore was finished, she made her way down a worn path to the safety of the bustling kitchen. Moses and Nellie came through the door carrying leftovers from the meal. Nellie set down her tray and pulled Early's trembling form against her bosom.

"He tried to attack me in the laundry." Anger shook Early as she fought the tears that already dripped from her eyes. "I left him stumbling in the dark and howling in pain until Moses took him away. Hopefully he won't be around for a while."

Moses grinned and nodded in agreement.

"I'm glad you escaped." Nellie rubbed the young woman's back, not needing to know who 'he' was.

"Escaped for now—but he's going to have a sore foot for a while." Early couldn't control the hysterical laughter that bubbled out. "I wonder how he will explain that to the master and mistress."

"I'm sure he will find something or someone to blame." Moses waved a chicken leg in front of her nose. "That young rooster deserves to stew for a while."

Nellie chuckled. "We better get the rest of that table cleared off before they find something else to blame us for."

Early brought the last of the serving dishes into the kitchen and then filled her plate before sitting down for a meal with Nellie and Moses. Washing dishes would follow soon enough, but in her exhausted state, it was nice to sit and replace some of her energy with the last of Nellie's crispy fried chicken, candied yams, and turnip greens. Luckily for the trio, the master's family had eaten lightly due to the tablecloth disaster, combined with a late tea when a neighbor had dropped by during the waning afternoon.

Moses rubbed his belly and smiled in satisfaction. "That was some of the best chicken I've had in a long time, Nellie."

"I couldn't agree more." Early sighed and added a hum of satisfaction. "I don't think I have room for another bite." In contradiction, she reached toward the breadbasket for a piece of cornpone.

Nellie's jolly laughter filled the room with her good humor. Early drizzled some honey mixed with molasses onto her dry piece of bread.

"It's 'most time for the washing up, honey, so don't be getting yourself too sweetened up with that sopping syrup. The master'll be wantin' his dishes to shine."

Moses grinned and stretched before launching into a well-known story. "Better use three waters to wash those dishes. That's the best way to keep them shinin'."

Early played along with the old storyteller's yarn. "So why would I want to use three waters when I can get away with just two?"

"Well, the story goes like this. There was this ole master that was visitin' up to his hill country relatives. They only had a small little ole log cabin but it was always neat and clean and shiny as a pin—especially the missus' fine china dishes. That woman always bragged about how she was able to bring those plates with her all the way from over the ocean. Now, she always fixed up some of her best vittles when her rich relative came to visit. There was grits and corn and plenty of black-eyed peas filled with ham hock and some wild mustard greens. On this one particular night, they sat around and even enjoyed an egg custard for dessert.

Then they got to talkin' and they kept up that there conversation until those perty plates were crusted with plenty of dried-on food. The visiting master, he was so sorry about it that he apologized to his kin and wondered if he would need to buy the lady some new dishes. The woman just laughed at him and said that was no problem 'cause she would just use three waters to get them clean.

Feeling ashamed of his self the master offered to send his man to fetch the water but the woman just waved her hand and hollered out, 'Here boy, here Three Waters.' Then an ole yeller dog walked into the room. Reachin' for the master's plate, she offered it to that dog and before long it was clean and shiny. Settin' it before him, the woman exclaimed that it was as clean as new and offered that feller a second helping of that custard. It only took a second for that ole master to grab his stomach and head for the great outdoors."

Early patted Moses' hand and then she reached over to pick up his plate. "Maybe we need to see if the hunting hounds can clean these dishes for you."

"I don't want no critters cleaning my eatin' utensils, but sometimes I have to fight the urge to mess with the young master's fixin's. I wouldn't mind doing something to his dinner plates though, 'specially after tonight."

Early nodded in agreement as her gaze shifted to the doors, hoping no one had heard Moses' bitter words. Nellie's shushing voice added to the tension that had suddenly invaded the warm room as all three occupants retreated to their own thoughts.

Early placed the dishes in the warm wash water and tried to not let her thoughts turn to the urge to do something like spit in the young master's soup when she served it tomorrow. Though it was a temptation, she inwardly straightened herself out and determined she was better than that. She wasn't always the best Christian, but she knew choosing not to harm the enemy was the right thing to do. She just prayed God would protect her from Sidney's advances. Rinsing the soap from the eating utensils and the troubling thoughts from her mind, she quickly dried the dishes and returned them to the sideboard for other meals.

~~~~~

The next morning Early noticed that the liquor cabinet was
~~~~~

once again secured, as she ran her dust rag across its shiny walnut casing. No drinks for Sidney today. Missy and Aunt 'Tilda had bemoaned Early's attack as they chatted during a quiet breakfast in her mistress's suite of rooms. They had prayed a prayer of thanksgiving that she'd been delivered from the human snake slithering around in the darkness. Then they had all laughed about how that serpent had been crushed by a rolling laundry cauldron.

Early chuckled, recalling their amusement. She wiped a few missed crumbs into her hand from the sideboard. They must have overlooked them last night. It was a blessing that Mistress Amanda hadn't spotted the messy sideboard this morning. She'd been looking for an excuse to punish Early.

Sidney staggered into the room. One foot swooshed across the floor in a knitted slipper while the other foot thumped in a dark leather boot. With a frown marring his face, he took in both the locked cabinet and Early's stunned face.

"Well, what do you know—a blessing and a curse. If I can't get any spirits, I can finally have my turn with a spirited girl." He pushed her against the wall between the cabinet and the sideboard, then rammed his hands into her hair.

Early's scream brought the whole household to the room.

Amanda fanned her heated face with a sandalwood fan. "What kind of display is this, Arthur? Have you no control of this slave girl?"

Aunt 'Tilda replied with a snort, "Have you no control of your son, woman?"

The two matrons glared at each other as Early pushed Sidney's hands away and ran to hide behind Missy's arm-crossed body.

"He has no right to mistreat anyone in this house." Missy's voice grew in volume as she raised a pointing finger to her stepbrother.

Papa Hollings' breath came fast and shallow as he joined the scene. His ashen face and spasmodic cough drew everyone's attention as he slumped into a chair.

"Arthur, are you all right?" Aunt 'Tilda dipped her handkerchief in a nearby bowl of flowers and dabbed water on her brother's face.

Amanda scented the air with sandalwood as she turned her unfolded fan toward his sweat-filled brow.

Papa pushed them both aside. "Just give me a moment's peace without everyone cackling like a bunch of chickens and I'll be fine." He stood up, and then collapsed back into the chair, allowing the fanning and dabbing to continue.

Amanda turned from her fluttering and glared at the younger mistress. "Take your little slave girl out of here before she kills my husband. I'll see to her punishment later. Sidney, get your father something to drink."

"Yes, Mother," Sidney replied and slunk toward the door.

Early's jaw dropped at the submissive tones coming from her attacker.

"And keep your hands off the help. You should know better. The future heir of this plantation should not be caught in a situation like this." Amanda pushed her son out of the room and then turned her glare toward the two young women.

Missy's hand tightened painfully around Early's fingers as they edged from the room. Early wondered at the declaration—was Sidney now the heir?

George

The next morning, Sidney thumped his way into the stable. Curses filled the air.

"Get my mare out here now. If I can't find what I need here at the plantation, I know a few places in town where I can get what I want."

George heard the commands but chose to not react. He kept wrapping the little mare's injured fetlock with the bandage soaked in liniment. If the poor horse went out today, chances were good she would not be coming back tonight. The whip marks on her rump had festered. Flies buzzed around the injury as she whisked them away with her tail. Her head hung down. George stood up and faced the angry man.

"She is not well, sir. Your horse cannot be ridden today without harming her."

"We'll see about that." Sidney's whip lashed across George's shoulder, leaving an open gash in his skin and shirt. "Move, man, and do as I ordered or you will receive more lashes."

"No."

The whip rang out again and again. George held in a cry. Blood trickled down his back. The horse shrieked in pain and snapped at Sidney as she broke loose from the stall and fled out of the barn. The startled attacker fell to the ground, giving George the opportunity to follow the fleeing mare.

Sidney rose from the ground and followed the two outside. He twirled the whip as he approached the two escapees. "Saddle her now."

A stern female voice entered the fray. "I don't think that would be a good idea, young man. That horse has lost all respect of you for the moment. She might just decide to take a bite out of you before she rolls over with you on her back." Aunt Matilda wagged her finger at Sidney. "My brother is going to be coming out of the house soon. If you have a brain in your head, you will choose a different mount and ride out of here before I tell him about your lack of horse sense. If the steed you take to town comes back looking like this one, my brother will be informed of your inability to deal with both man and beast."

George saw Sidney clamp his jaw shut and turn toward the barn. The ailing mare limped to the edge of the paddock. The sound of tromping horseshoes sounded from the doorway. Old John stood silently holding the reins to another horse. The old man smirked as he boosted the young master into the saddle. The barely broken stallion's ears lay back as he bared his teeth and took off with a jerk.

Chapter Eight

Early

That same morning, Master Hollings had called for a meeting between Aunt Matilda, Missy, and Early. He'd asked everyone to wear comfortable clothing for a walk, but Early wondered if he had the strength for an outing. His breathing still seemed labored, filling her with the fear of an unknown future.

Aunt Matilda stood by the barn, talking to George as the other three stepped out from the back of the plantation home. When the handsome man turned away to tend to a limping horse, she noticed rips in his shirt and wondered if the horse had done him harm. She hoped not. Aunt Matilda didn't look happy as she turned away from the scene and joined the others. Early raised her eyebrows in question, but the aunt shook her head to dismiss further inquiry.

They headed down a path leading them toward the morning sun. The master leaned heavily on his sister. He paused from time to time to catch his breath, his eyes looking toward the heavens. Cloud-filled skies reflected a warm pink and purple glow. Early stepped along the well-known trail, a few steps behind the others. She'd accompanied Missy to her mother's grave many times over the years and helped collect wildflowers to place near the chiseled stone marker. When they reached the burial grounds, Master Hollings led them to another grave, grown over with green moss and weeds.

He leaned over and brushed at the moss-covered gravestone. A cough shook his body and rattled in his chest as he stirred the dust from the faded headstone. "Guess it won't be long until I'm joining my wayward brother in the soil. Hopefully I'll make it to the good place, but I'm not sure about brother Jeremiah's soul."

Early lingered behind Missy, wondering why they brought her on the family outing. At least Mistress Amanda and Sidney had not joined the others. Mist fell from the overcast sky and left glistening drops on buds pushing their way through rotted leaves and hopeful shoots of green grass awakening to moisture and warmer temperatures.

The master cleared his throat and turned to look at Aunt Matilda. "I know there have been speculations about the relationship between Missy and Early all their lives."

"You haven't been fooling any of us, brother. It's about time you owned up to your indiscretions." Aunt sniffed and wagged a bony finger.

"That's where you are wrong, my dear sister."

"Harrumph!" Aunt 'Tilda fisted her hands and moved them to her hips. Her eyes focused an accusing glare on the master.

"Unfortunately, our brother was a lot like Sidney. My daughter has a cousin, not a sister, as you no doubt thought to be the case." He cleared his throat and shifted his gaze between the two younger women. His face wasn't the only one that paled at the announcement.

Silence filled the air, except for a distant robin's chirp. No one spoke, not even Aunt Matilda, who seemed to be praying.

Early shifted her gaze and stared into Missy's matching hazel orbs. Understanding filled her heart. She'd always felt like they were almost sisters, but the idea of being cousins had never crossed her thoughts.

Missy looked like she might swoon. Early felt close to doing the same, but her looser garments kept her breathing, unlike Missy's tightly corseted waist. Even Aunt Matilda started fanning her face and gaped at her brother. Then her features changed.

"We cannot let history repeat itself. We need to protect both our girls, and I have a plan." Aunt 'Tilda's voice grew strong.

"I understand. I may not like your plan, but it may be best for all." Master Hollings' troubled eyes surveyed the group as he steadied himself by leaning on the cemetery's iron fence. For the first time in her life, Early looked her master straight in the eye.

Missy

That evening, Missy stared into her mirror and looked through her tears at the reflected hazel eyes. She'd always wanted a sister, and in the recesses of her mind had wondered if her relationship with Early held the answer. She'd never considered having a cousin. Aunt Matilda never had a child of her own. Aunt Mary Etta raised her children in Ohio. She'd never met the much older northern cousins. Perhaps she would someday.

Papa never mentioned Uncle Jeremiah during her growing years, other than saying he died tragically in a horse riding accident. Now she knew why he'd avoided telling her more about his brother. At least she knew Papa was an honorable man and not Early's father. She struggled with that thought but chose not to dwell on the matter. She wondered if her birth mother had known the truth or had only suffered from the gossip surrounding Early's mother. What did poor Early think about the information they'd learned this morning? The girl had a pure heart, almost biblically pure. How could she be the offspring of such a scoundrel? She'd had a godly mother, who'd given them both a heavenly heritage. That was how she was so good-natured. Why did her cousin have to endure slavery?

She left her room and marched down the stairs, seeking Papa. She heard his voice in the library and headed in that direction.

Aunt Matilda sat in the chair across from his desk. Her hands faced the sky. "Arthur, you have to let the girl go, for her own good. We can't have our own blood relatives in the throes of slavery. You've held onto this for too long. Help me make things right."

"But Missy is attached to the girl. It would break her heart for me to separate them," Papa rasped out.

Missy stepped into the room, feeling braver than Queen Esther. It was a new feeling and power flowed into her raised head and voice. "Then don't separate us, Papa. It sounds like you may be giving my heritage here at Holly Plantation away to Sidney anyway. Let the two of us go, before Sidney ruins one or the other of us like Jeremiah ruined Early's mother. Give me a portion of the inheritance that should be mine and allow us the freedom to join our aunts in the north."

God had given her the words to speak, many of them reminiscent of memorized verses from childhood. Her heart felt torn as she looked at the father she loved. She saw from the gray tint of his cheeks that his time on earth might be limited. If he let them go, it might be the last time she saw him alive. She put her hands to her cheeks to cover the tears that flowed and sank into a tapestry-covered chair that matched the one her aunt occupied.

Papa cleared his voice and reached across the desk for her

hand. "I understand. I hate to see you leave here, but your aunt and I were just discussing the matter. Unfortunately, all my funds are tied up in recent purchases and this year's future crops. I don't have much to share with you."

"Then give me Early as my inheritance. I'll be eighteen soon. Let me have her papers and the right to set her free when we reach Aunt Mary Etta's home." She took her father's offered hand in both of hers and looked deeply into his eyes, searching for a positive answer.

Papa released her hand and pulled a desk drawer open. He pulled out a sheaf of papers and sorted through them until he found what he looked for. With a few swirls of his pen, he pushed the paper toward Missy. "She is yours. It's the least I can do. I will miss you, child. You have been a gift to me from your mother." Tears coursed down his pasty cheeks as he came around the desk and hugged his daughter.

Aunt Matilda's voice broke through their tears. "Now that you've settled that matter, we need to talk about the horse and carriage you were going to sell me."

"Yes, sister. I have a very gentle mare that I have in mind. She's great with both a small carriage and for riding. She's performing quite well for our new groomsman."

At the mention of the horseman, Missy's heart sank. He would make the perfect companion for Early. If they moved on, would Early be able to find someone who cared for her? "Papa, is the carriage going to come with a driver?"

"I'm very adept at handling a horse, young lady." Aunt 'Tilda crossed her arms.

"I don't doubt that you are, but I think the groomsman who has handled the horse might be an asset to our travels." Missy paused before continuing in a quiet voice. "I think he might add to our safety, especially Early's. I doubt she will be allowed to sleep in our room when we stop at an inn each night."

"Are you saying he would sleep in the room with Early? I don't think that is proper." Aunt's indignation filled the room. Papa nodded in agreement.

"But what if they were married? I happen to know that they seem like a good match. I've enjoyed overhearing their conversations on several carriage rides."

Papa shook his head. "While this sounds like a good plan, I can spare your maid — I mean cousin — but I need a good man with the horses. I can't afford to replace him at this time."

Missy sagged into her chair.

"What if I bought him?" Matilda looked disgusted with herself, but she sat up in her chair. "I never wanted to own a slave, but this will only be until we can get them both up north. Then I'll set him free, too."

"He doesn't come cheap. You may not have that kind of money." Papa transformed into the businessman he'd always been as he named a steep price.

"You can't be serious. My funds will be seriously depleted." Aunt's face begged for a better deal.

"I am. It's only slightly higher than what I paid for him." His eyes narrowed as he looked at his sister. The two bargainers glared at each other for a few moments.

"Please, Papa. Do this for Early, your niece."

His shoulders lowered. "I can come down a little, not much more. I have to replace him. Old John isn't getting any younger."

"I'm glad you came to your senses, Arthur. I shouldn't be doing this, but the time has come to stand up for what is right — even if I have to do a wrong to correct it." 'Tilda reached for her brother's hand and sealed the deal.

Papa searched his drawer once more and signed George's paper over to his sister. "I just have one request. Do not tell anyone about your plan to set them free. It would not be wise for Amanda or Sidney to have that knowledge."

Papa coughed. For a few moments he seemed lost in thought, and then he turned his attention to Missy. "I'll arrange for the preacher to stay after worship on Sunday for their vows. You had best get your cousin ready for the changes that will be happening in the next few weeks."

He dismissed his daughter and turned to his sister. "We have some details to work out before your departure."

Missy bustled up the stairs and into her room, where she found Early mending clothing.

Early

"Aunt 'Tilda and I have decided you're going to marry that young buck and you're going to be happy about it or else." Missy's determined voice hinted at both the power she had over her slave and the concern that she had for the young woman who had been her near sister for their lifetime.

Early ground her teeth. Her fingers stabbed the mending needle into the petticoat she was stitching back together. "Don't I have something to say about this, cousin?"

"Trust me, Early, it will be for the best. Besides, I can tell you both like each other. Since we're going to be traveling together, you're going to need someone to protect you. Most inns won't let you stay with me. I'm sure you don't want to even consider what might happen to you in whatever quarters they put slaves for the night."

Early spoke through clenched teeth. "He's not a young buck. His name is George and you know it. Now, maybe you're seeing something that I can't, because he certainly hasn't said anything about being in love with me. One time I thought he might care, but whenever I start thinking that, he scoots away and starts talking about—well, never mind what he starts talking about. I don't think he'll agree to it."

"George won't have much choice. I've already pointed out to Papa that he would be a good match for you and it will work out perfectly for us to have our driver and lady's maid along for the trip."

"How could you do this to me, Missy? I've stood by you all these years and obeyed you to the best of my ability and now you want to cast me off like—like a slave."

"I'm sorry, Early, but it's for your own good. I wish it was only me doing this to you, but there's more to it than you or I really know or understand. Most of this plan isn't mine. It has something to do with an agreement between Aunt 'Tilda and Papa. We can't tell you everything, but I think you'll be all right in the end. Papa's already arranged for the wedding to take place down at the church on Sunday afternoon, so you better be thinking about which dress of mine you want to borrow for the ceremony."

George

"You have to be joshing me! I can't be marrying anybody. You know I've got plans." George hissed the last part of his tirade as he vented to Old John. Banging loudly on a heated piece of iron caused the horseshoe to split into two pieces. One fell to the ground with a *thunk* while the hammer clunked against the one still sitting on the huge black anvil.

"I'm only telling you what I overheard when I drove the master and his sister, Miss 'Tilda around. They gots plans for you and they involve that little pampered filly you been looking at with your big brown eyes." John pranced around the stable, holding out an imaginary skirt, and fluttered his eyelashes at the frustrated young man.

"Early is not a horse and she doesn't act like that around me, so you better quit your dancing around."

"I noticed you didn't leave when the owl was hootin' the other week. I figured that maybe a certain maid might a been the one keepin' you from heading out. I heard there was a couple of fellows that took out from the McDonald place that night."

"Yeah, I heard that too. I also heard they didn't get very far so it was good I didn't go—seems like the road to freedom doesn't work too well this far south."

"Maybe marrying the little woman will harness your desire to wander. It ain't too bad here compared to a lot of places."

"It could be worse but that still don't make it right for a man to own another and decide things, like who should be hopping the broom with them."

"No need to worry about gettin' a broom. They was talking about a real church wedding for the two of you, so you oughta be looking good when they come to take you away. I'm thinking you better be polishin' the buttons on your drivin' livery if you know what's good for you."

"I don't want to do this, John. It don't fit my plans even if she is a pretty gal. I want my freedom, and dragging her along would just cause problems."

"I could deal with a problem as perty as her. She's one good lookin' gal."

"Was your Sally as pretty as Early, John?"

"You're trying to change the subject, ain't ya? Sally was quite a gal." The wistful smile on old John's face spoke of the love that he had for his departed wife. "But it's your chance now, son, so why don't ya admit that you like the girl and enjoy what the master has planned?"

"I'd like to, but I can't put another family through what happened to mine, when there's a chance they'll be sold off whenever the master wants some spending money."

"So you're talking about having little ones already." John laughed and threw an elbow into George's side.

"Not gonna happen if I can help it."

George stomped away from the chuckling old man and entered the first stall he approached. It didn't help that the stall contained one of the breeding mares who was due to foal within the next week or so. The poor horse's distended sides were evidence of her discomfort as he slowly led the beast from her confinement and turned her out into the paddock. Cleaning her stall went quickly and then he completed all the other mucking chores in record time.

Missy

Missy rarely ventured down to where Early normally slept. Today the two young women sat on the edge of the simple rope bed, sorting through her cousin's meager belongings and packing them into a calico pillowcase. They added her few chemises, petticoats, two dark servant's dresses and a worn quilt to the stash. Early's mother had stitched the top of the quilt out of scraps of cloth from her young mistress's childhood gowns. The back had been pieced together from the brown cloth used for her mother's serving dresses. It held memories of picnics on the lawn and huddling together on stormy nights. Missy hugged the blanket close before pushing it into the cloth case.

"Your mother was the best thing that ever happened to me."

"Guess you can call her your aunt now, just as I can call 'Tilda my aunt." Early stood and looked around the room. "I can't say I will miss Nellie's snores. I'm really glad you've shared your balcony and room with me for a while this spring. I will miss being with you in this old house. I only wish..."

The sound of someone tramping down the stairs echoed through the basement area as Sidney called out their names. Without saying a word, they nodded toward the fireplace where Nellie sometimes did her cooking when it was too hot to cook upstairs. Pushing aside what looked like part of the oven bricks, they snuck into the tiny cellar room where they'd hidden as children. A single shaft of light kept them from total darkness. They heard him stomp across the dirt floor and pause near their hiding place.

"I smell lavender. They should be around here somewhere. Pretty maids ripe for the picking..." His feet shuffled away as he muttered, "I want to make one of them mine before they get married off to someone else. I like my women pure."

Missy stifled her gasp and hugged her cousin closer. Marriage would mean safety for Early. She hoped they all made it out of town before Sidney could do either of them harm. The two girls waited in the near darkness for a long stretch of time before slipping from their hiding place. Using the servants' stairway, they entered Missy's suite and locked the door behind them.

Aunt 'Tilda's off-tune warbling reached their ears from the neighboring room. Missy stepped next door to lock her aunt's door also.

"Aunt Matilda, we've had another near miss with that scoundrel. If we hadn't hidden in a — a special place, then he might have done us harm."

"Hmmm. This is not good. I think maybe it is time for Arthur to send that scallywag on an errand until we can be off, or at least until Early's wedding day."

Chapter Nine

Early

Thankful that the master had sent Sidney out of town, Early allowed herself permission to seek refuge in the fact that at least he would not be present at the wedding. She donned the pretty bonnet Missy purchased on her first ride to town with George. It brought a blush of anticipation that spread throughout her heart and soul.

Maybe George didn't love her as much as he loved the thought of freedom, but that was all right. She'd opened her mind to the idea of him as her protector, and maybe more as time provided. Smoothing down the simple cotton gown she had chosen from Missy's plainer dresses made her feel proud to be dressed properly for the church wedding taking place later in the afternoon. The two young women descended the mahogany stairs together, heads held high. Warm air and chirping birds greeted them as they stepped from the house.

Mistress Amanda sniffed at their appearance, but for once kept her thoughts to herself. Moses helped the master's family into the carriage and then turned to take Early to her place on the seat with George.

Stepping up to the carriage seat had become routine. Moses extended his hand. "Here you go, Miss Early, up to sit with your handsome groom."

"Thank you, Moses." Early timidly smiled up at George as he extended his strong right arm to hoist her through the air. Instead of the warmth she expected, she saw a raging storm sweeping across his face, punctuated by scowling eyebrows. Huffing, she raised her chin and gave her unwelcoming groom a dismissive look of her own. "You could at least pretend you liked me a little on our wedding day." She hadn't been much happier than he, but had opted to have a positive attitude. It wasn't like they had any other choice.

"No need to pretend about that, Miss Early. Maybe I care too much and that's not a good thing." He shook the reins. His eyes focused forward.

"Well, you better make the best of it because I'm glad that we're going to at least get a good heaven blessed wedding." When there was no answer to her comment, she tried again. "Wonder what white folks church will be like this morning? I'm going to miss hearing Moses tell his Bible stories out under the trees today. Did you know he learned most of his tales while he was serving the family during their own devotions?" As she rambled on about Bible stories, the only acknowledgement that her groom listened came from an occasional grunt or nod.

A dip in the road caused the couple to jostle against each other. George wrapped one arm around Early as he heaved a deep sigh. "It's not you I'm upset with, darling. I'm scared. Scared about the future, scared about if we have — well, I'm just scared. Besides that, I don't like being forced to do this when I didn't have a chance to ask you myself." His half-grin sent a message to Early that spoke of the words he refused to say aloud.

Leaning into his side, Early took hope from that one *darling* word, which slipped out from his lips. "Well, you better not be too scared because I've been told we are doing this for my protection. I'm counting on you being my hero."

"Don't know how much help I'll be unless we can make it to Canaan someday."

Stiffening next to him with her own fears, Early found that her desire to talk had fled. Her mind turned to thoughts of the promised trip with Missy. What dangers might they face on that trip? Fleeing to Canaan would be dangerous, but staying here with Sydney would not be any safer. Her thoughts spun like the spring tornado that had damaged the chicken coop a few years ago. Doubts and fears waged war in her mind for the rest of the trip to church.

George reined the horses to a stop and tied off the brake before leaping down from the high seat. He turned to catch Early as she tumbled into his arms. The fresh smell of laundered clothing mingled with the sweet scent of hair oil as their arms wrapped around each other. The master's rasping cough brought them back to reality. George dropped his hands from her waist. Early placed a hand over her pounding heart as her groom abruptly turned to open the door for the Hollings family.

As George performed his duties, Early took the time to clear her head. She gazed at the various conveyances scattered across the crowded lot near the imposing brick church. An older woman stood near a man who was busy hobbling his master's horses. She waved Early over and grabbed the younger woman's hands.

"Have you been to a white service before, honey?" When Early shook her head, the woman leaned closer and whispered advice. "I'm thinking it's gonna be a little quieter than you're used to. Don't go hallelujahin' out loud or Amenin' when you feel like it."

"Why not?"

"It's jest not done at this kind of church. Now don't you worry 'bout a thing. You and your man can come sit quietly in the balcony with me and mine. We'll think our glory be's to ourselves. It's not as tiresome as it sounds and the preacher man ain't half bad."

Early thought about denying the fact that George wasn't exactly her man yet, but her mind stumbled when the object of her thoughts appeared at her side and possessively threaded his arm through hers. Following the friendly older couple, they entered a side door and climbed a steep flight of stairs to the balcony at the rear of the church. Other families slid over to make room for the new couple. Names were offered and heads nodded in welcome. Early found herself tucked in closely to George as they squeezed in with the other worshippers. Why hadn't she thought to borrow one of Missy's sandalwood fans? She suddenly felt very warm. George must be feeling the heat too, if his quietly hissed breath was any indication. The fact that he had to put his arm behind her on the back of the pew to make more room did not help one bit.

As the service began, the rumbling sound of lengthy pipes reverberated through the building as music, unlike anything Early had ever heard or seen before, rang out with a great formal hymn. Feeling the vibrations coursing through her body, Early felt like the great Almighty had sent His angels to bring the end of the world.

The elderly woman leaned over and patted Early's hand as she whispered, "Ain't that sound something? It's jest an ole pipe organ bellowing out a fine white man's song of worship."

Trying to relax as the service proceeded proved difficult, due to the handsome man sitting next to her, trying hard not to show any emotion, and the music that shook her from head to toe. When a familiar hymn hummed from the great musical beast, Early warbled out a semblance of a tune. In quiet contrast, the minister's prayer time brought a balm to her soul. However, the sermon about the responsibilities of husbands and wives seemed aimed right at her heart. She hoped George understood the man. His squirms indicated he clearly heard the message God sent to their ears.

George

George bounced his leg as he tried ignoring the sermon. That preacher's tongue showed him no mercy. Once the ceremony bound him to this woman, it would be his God-given duty to care for her. He knew in one part of his divided mind that he wanted her with all his heart, but he did not want to deal with both of them tied to slavery for the rest of their lives. There was no way he would bring children into this world—even if it took every bit of his self-control. No child should have to experience the loss he had endured.

When the service finally ended, George gathered Early's hand in his as they carefully descended the staircase. His heart fought with his will, all the while knowing he really had no choice. They would be married. The master had made the decision for them. There was no option, as long as slavery existed in his life. He would protect the woman he had started to care for in more ways than he wanted to admit, but someday he would find a way to make them free.

While the churchgoers cleared the sanctuary, Early and George lingered in the shadows near the side door. Aunt Matilda, Missy and Master Hollings slowly wove their way through the crowd and waited with the couple until the minister completed his parting blessings. Amanda joined a group of women under shady trees. Her back faced the waiting couple, Master Hollings, 'Tilda, and Missy.

Finally, the minister clasped their master's hand and tipped an invisible hat toward Missy as George and Early stood in silence. "So Master Hollings, it seems like you have a fine-looking couple ready to be wed." Early stole a peek at George, then she averted her face. A shy smile spread to her lips and warmed something deep inside of his soul. He reached for her hand and a peaceful acceptance about what would take place flowed from their connection.

"Yes sir, a fine couple at that. This is my daughter's personal girl, and the man is one of my finest groomsmen. I'm sure they'll have some handsome offspring in the future." Master Hollings seemed to regret his words, which made no sense to George. Arthur Hollings would be disappointed if he planned on them giving him a bunch of children to enslave.

George stiffened, but otherwise kept his thoughts contained as the master's words seemed to compare him and Early to the prize horses in the plantation's barn. Though he loved those brood mares, he did not like the way the master compared the two of them to the animals on the plantation. As Early placed her other hand on their joined ones, he took a calming breath and vowed that he would love this woman with his whole heart, but not his body.

"First things first," the minister advised as he led them to a side room where he had the couple place their x's in the church record book. Missy carefully spelled out their names and then signed as one of the witnesses. Her father's scrawling signature served as a second witness. Missy's knowing wink as her father bent over the paper acknowledged that she knew Early understood the printed words as well as she did, but that it had to remain a secret. Once they got up north, George hoped Early would teach her new husband to write his own name, too.

Leading the couple outside under a grove of trees, the ceremony that sealed their lives together took place before God, Matilda, Master Hollings, and Missy. As the closing words pronounced them husband and wife, the minister encouraged the couple to seal their vows with a kiss.

Early lifted her face to George's. He expected to offer a simple peck on the lips with their small wedding party looking on. However, as their lips met, expectations exploded. His mouth met hers with a passion that surprised them both. Early sighed. Missy and Aunt 'Tilda giggled as Papa Hollings cleared his throat. The master's cleared throat grew into a rasping cough. The noise made George straighten and stare at his bride in awe when he finally broke contact from the long kiss.

Fighting for control, George snapped away. He bowed to the master and led the group toward the carriage. The minister's chuckle followed the little entourage as he wished God's blessings upon their life together.

Early

Early clasped her hands together as George closed the cabin door. What would this night bring? Old Nellie had told her what to expect, but she wasn't real clear on some things. He pointed to a pallet on one side of the small building.

"You can have my bed. I'll sleep by the door. At least I can protect you tonight. I'll protect you from myself and from Sidney. There won't be any children between us until we reach freedom. We got to be ready, and we don't need anything holding us back. Do you understand?"

She didn't understand, but sighed in relief at the prospect of not having to participate in the unknown. But then again, was she so unlovely that he couldn't love her? Her thoughts swirled in confusion. She'd given up her warm lodging off the kitchen for a leaky shack and a husband who didn't want to be one.

Ginny Interlude

Ginny admired the holiday wreaths hanging from doors in the historic part of the small Alabama town. The Southern Charm Christmas tour had been a combination present, to both her and Mom. The warm journey south provided a chance to research the area where Missy might have lived, and enjoy a break from cold northern weather. They'd toured several houses already, including one with a high cupola and winding staircase.

She stepped closer when the tour guide stopped in front of the ancient Alabama church and began talking about weddings. When he mentioned marriage records found in the old church for couples in slavery, she waved her hand and got his attention.

"I thought those held in slavery did not have weddings in white churches."

"That is true in many cases, but in this town there were many who brought enslaved couples in for a Christian marriage. It was also common practice at this meeting house for many black people to sit in the balcony and participate in services every Sunday."

Ginny pulled her worn spiral notebook from her deep purse and took notes. She could hardly wait until she got home and compared it with the wedding account in Missy's journal. Her own journey between North and South would be over tomorrow when she and Mom headed home on a jet. A much quicker trip than Missy, Early, George, and Aunt Matilda would have endured in the past, when they had to leave the only home the two young women had ever known.

Missy

Missy sat alone on a bench under the shade of their largest live oak tree and studied the only home she'd ever known. Spanish moss whispered above her head when a small breeze brought some relief from summer heat. She reached for her box of sharpened pencils and added details to the drawing she'd started yesterday. The scent of roses blooming filled the air. A mother she never knew had planted the pink blooms. She mourned that mother and the nanny who had raised her as her own. She missed her lifelong companion, Early.

Another servant had entered her room the last two mornings to help her get ready for the day. The same unhappy looking young woman had helped her change for bed each evening. Guilt had flowed down her spine as she thought of the sadness that emanated from the new maid. She couldn't save everyone, could she? She didn't even know the girl's name. Her stepmother had forbidden her to befriend the servant, who reacted in terror when Missy tried to communicate. Amanda must have given the young woman strict instructions.

Amanda decided that since Early had married, the time had come to implement her changes in the household. Little did the older woman know that things were about to change drastically, but those plans had to be kept secret for now. She hoped Early enjoyed being married to the man she admired. Her newly discovered cousin and former maid had helped in the kitchen before, so being assigned there full-time may not have been too big of an adjustment.

The change had taken an interesting turn when Sidney arrived before yesterday's evening meal. When Papa mentioned Early's marriage, Sidney had clamped his mouth shut and turned toward Missy with a gleam in his eyes. His look had raised chill bumps on her arms, which cooled the hot summer air like a winter snowstorm. She'd stood and retreated to her locked room until the new maid came to help her undress for the night. Then she'd tightly twisted her door key in the lock after the girl left. This morning, she'd dared to enjoy being outside for a while, hoping Sidney would not attempt to do anything in plain view of the house.

"Hello, darling." Sidney's slimy voice made Missy's pulse jump in fear as he stepped from behind the oak tree. She'd been too distracted to notice his approach and a ripple of dread coursed down her back.

She forced composure into her voice when she answered him with a frown. "I am not anyone's darling. You need to leave me alone or you will answer for your unwanted behavior."

"Who would I be answering to, woman? I happen to know that our parents are in town at the moment, and we are all alone. They took your married maid and her husband with them. I sent Moses and the kitchen help on an errand that will keep them busy for a while. No one else will dare to defy me if they know what is good for them."

"What about my aunt? You know she won't let you get away with this." She hugged her journal and pencils to her chest.

"Let's just say she may have had a little sleeping powder slipped into her morning tea." His sneer turned into something more fearsome. He stepped closer and she smelled the liquor on his breath.

Missy moved to the edge of her seat. Aunt 'Tilda had complained about the tea Sidney had served her this morning. They'd both been surprised when he brought over her cup filled to the brim. Aunt had commented about too much sugar and something not tasting right.

She set her drawing aside and pulled out her pen knife. Missy pretended to sharpen one of the Thoreau pencils her father had given her. The side of the pencil was marked with a number one. She rarely used it. The lead was too hard. Sharpening it would take time, if the already pointed pencil had required it. She needed a few moments to think about what she would do if Sidney did try to grab her. Most of the slaves now lived in fear of his whip. She was on her own. The knife might prove valuable.

Sidney wrenched the pen knife from her hand, threw it to the ground, pulled her to her feet and drew her tightly into his embrace, pinching her arms close to her body. Her fingers wrapped around the pencil.

"Let. Me. Go."

"What are you going to do? Whip me with your little pencil? It will crumble to pieces like any other pencil. You're going to be my woman, whether you like it or not." He pushed her back against the oak and grabbed the side of her skirt.

Missy fisted the pencil and plunged it into the nearest part of his body. His scream matched the ripping of cloth with the hole torn through his pants. The pencil in her hand dripped with drops of blood as Sidney rolled on the ground, cursing and crying like a baby.

"Guess this pencil is mightier than any sword. You must not have heard about Mr. Thoreau's advances in making very hard pencils." Her voice sounded strangled at first, but triumph over the enemy filled her as she gathered her journal, pen knife, and the rest of her pencils.

As Sidney struggled to get back to his feet, she trembled and ran as fast as she could for the safety of her room. Once there, she locked the door to her room and the adjoining one where Aunt 'Tilda gently snored. She shoved several pieces of furniture in front of each door and climbed into the bed with her aunt.

"Protect us, Heavenly Father."

Chapter Ten

Missy

Aunt 'Tilda seethed with anger after waking from her drug-induced nap, which had lasted for the rest of the day and into the next morning. When she could walk without tipping, she stomped from their rooms, telling her niece to lock the doors behind her. Missy's empty stomach rumbled, reminding her that she'd refused to let the maid enter at yesterday's mealtimes, in fear that Sidney might be outside. She paced around the room as she waited for her aunt to return from a confrontation between brother and sister. She lifted desperate prayers until she heard her aunt outside the door, asking to enter.

'Tilda's determined voice filled the room once Missy opened the door.

"Melissa, your father has granted permission for us to start our travels tomorrow. In light of Sidney's advances yesterday, we think it might be best to be on our way before something else happens." Aunt Matilda closed the door behind her. She propped open her trunk that had been sitting at the foot of her bed and began to fold clothing into its depth.

Missy's heart jerked at the idea of leaving her father forever. She hated that Sidney had forced her father's hand, but relief washed over her shoulders at the thought of being out of his reach. Thinking about Papa's sallow cheeks and raspy voice made her realize she might not see him again. Would Amanda offer him help if he needed it? She could only hope. Surely Papa had seen something in her that made him want to marry her. It certainly had not been her son, though he seemed to have bewitched Papa with his smooth words, until recently.

A few moments later, she heard a rap at the door. Fear snaked up her back until she heard Moses identify himself.

"I've got some food for you, Missy. I know you got to be hungry."

"Are you alone?"

"Yes, ma'am. The doctor's already come and confined the young master to his bed." His laughter resounded through the solid door. "I'll be waiting around outside your door for a while. He won't be bothering you while I'm on guard."

Missy opened the door and took the plate of food from his hands. "Thank you, Moses. I will rest easy knowing you are keeping watch."

As she ate the nourishing stew, guilt plagued her. She hated knowing she'd hurt another person, but there hadn't been much choice. Sidney would have done her more harm than she'd inflicted on him.

Her thoughts drifted to Early's arranged marriage to George. She wondered if they had done wrong by forcing the two to wed. Her newly recognized cousin had barely spoken to her since the nuptials last Sunday.

Aunt snapped a chemise in the air before folding it into her trunk. "Choose your wardrobe carefully. You will need sensible clothing for travel. If you decide to stay up north with us, you won't find many occasions to wear any hooped skirts."

"I'll see what I have that works." Missy put down her spoon and stepped into the adjoining room. A rhythmic knock at the door let her know Early stood outside. When her cousin entered the room, she carried a basket of freshly launder clothing. Papa must have put his foot down and returned her maid to her former duties after Aunt's earlier visit. "Welcome back." Early nodded with her eyes downcast. Missy sighed. "No need to put the laundry away. We're going to start our trip tomorrow, so we'll be loading up a travel trunk with things we need."

"We?"

Missy huffed at the one-word reply. "Yes, we. Aunt Matilda, you, me, and your George. We're going to leave for the trip we talked about. Now help me pick out some simple travel clothing."

Early's sad eyes met Missy's. "Papa Hollings? Will he...?"

"I don't know, but he told Aunt we needed to leave before Sidney recovers."

"I understand." A fleeting grin passed over her face. "I heard you made sure he would not be bothering either of us for a while. I'm proud of you."

Moses tapped at the door and then tugged a travel trunk into the room. "Heard you'd be needin' this." He nodded to Early, then headed to the door with a sad expression on his face.

"Good-bye, Moses." Early swiped at her eyes with her shoulder as she watched the old servant close the door on his way out. Missy heard her cousin sigh as the girl turned her focus back to placing folded undergarments into the trunk. "Which dresses do you think you would like packed for the trip?"

"Something simple, this green one for sure. The lavender one has always been a favorite for everyday wear." Missy paused and wrapped her arms around her cousin, sharing her tears. "Pick out a couple of my dresses for yourself, because things are going to be different on this trip." She picked up a small satchel and filled it with her journal and pencils. "You never know when these might come in handy again." Both young women giggled. Missy stepped back and searched the room. "Have you seen the little pouch you sewed for me to wear under my garments? I might want to put a few keepsakes in there for safekeeping."

Holly Plantation

Dear Mary Etta,

Tomorrow our journey will begin. It has been a trying time. Both girls have faced the unseemly advances of Arthur's stepson. Those actions made it clear to our brother that changes must happen to protect the girls. He agreed to send them with me as I journey your way. I have had to make a hard choice and do something that I would never have dreamed of doing since the day I married my Frederick. I am now the owner of a slave. I had no other way to save our dear niece's new husband. Yes, one of them is married. Arthur gifted Early's papers to Melissa as a gift for her upcoming eighteenth birthday. That will give her the right to offer her cousin freedom once we are out of states that embrace slavery. We arranged for Early to marry a young man in order to discourage Sidney. It seems he is only interested in pure young women.

Unfortunately, after their marriage he turned his attention toward our Melissa, who stood up for herself in a way that made our brother recognize the problem. I didn't have the heart to separate our Early from her man. Arthur might have gifted him to us had circumstances been different, but Amanda's expensive lifestyle required that I pay dearly for his ownership. Securing a horse and conveyance has also depleted my monies, but I think we will be able to make it your way. I hope you will have the heart to take us all in when we arrive from what may turn into a dangerous journey.

I am enclosing a note for Samuel filled with poetry for the Cause.

With love,
Matilda

Samuel

Samuel eagerly reached for the papers once his aunt finished reading her own letter.

Mary Etta's eyebrows rose in curiosity. She chuckled as she pulled them out of his reach. "It seems your interest in my niece has grown since our last letters arrived."

"Her poems are good for the Cause. Don't read more into the situation than you should." He prayed the Lord didn't think him a liar for the words that fell from his lips. "I can't believe your sister owns a slave. Surely there had to be another way." He hoped the distraction would take her mind off of romance.

"She must not have had a choice, or she would have taken it. Now, how badly do you want your poetry?" Mary Etta held the papers close to her nose and inhaled.

He held his hand out and frowned until she handed them over with a knowing grin.

Dear Samuel Woodson,

Aunt 'Tilda tells me that we will be going on an adventure that may involve an eventual meeting between the two of us. So, for now I will no longer attempt to send missives your way. Papa has gifted me with a new set of Thoreau pencils for recording our travels in my journal. I may have done some damage to my other set. He planned to give me the new set for one of my birthday gifts, so I will celebrate a little early. This note will be my last ink-stained correspondence for a while.

Papa's final gift to me is more precious than any I have ever received. He has given my cousin Early's papers to me so that she can be free once we find our way north. You might remember her as a slave who served refreshments at the wedding, but Papa has revealed our true relationship. I had suspected a blood relationship but did not know the truth. She has always been like a sister and now I know she is even more. She is my kinsman, the daughter of an uncle I never knew and my beloved nanny. In the future she will be my equal.

Sincerely Yours,
Melissa Hollings

He tried to stop his reaction to the words 'sincerely yours,' but his mind had other plans. She was not his and never would be, but his memory traveled back to the dance they had shared at her father's wedding reception. She'd been his for a few moments as they'd swept away their differences while the music flew them into a world of their own. Her soft hair had brushed against his chin and made him forget his vow to never marry again. When the music stopped and a female slave stepped near to offer him refreshment, the spell had been abruptly broken as he'd looked at the serving woman with eyes and face so like the woman he held.

Missy's talk of not liking the way she lived had loosened his tongue at the wedding. He'd laid down the challenge of using writing as a tool. It had been a dangerous choice. That night, she could have betrayed his purpose to her family. She didn't. Now she followed through with poetry and purpose as she began her new journey. He flattened her page filled with poems on his worktable and studied the first one.

Sailing Away

Four travelers set sail today,
Across a changing tide.
A queenly captain guides their way,
Three sailors at her side.

They ride the waves to unknown lands,
Wond'ring if they'll see,

A purpose for their open hands,
Where each of them is free.

The horseman guides our ship along,
Through waters smooth and tossed,
His rumbling voice is filled with song,
When we are safe or lost.

The humble maid takes care of all,
With dressing, bath, or tea.
She does each task without a call,
Of pain or misery.

The poet bard will keep the log,
Recording each event.
She takes her notes through storm and fog,
Until her ink is spent.

The queenly captain points the ship,
To welcome bay or shore.
She finds no need for cane or whip,
To ask her crew for more.

Samuel re-read the short letter and poem. The poetry clearly symbolized the journey of the little group, perhaps too clearly. He could not print it as an article for his paper. The poem would give hints about the journey that might jeopardize their safety. He reached for his aunt's hands and together they prayed for safe travels. Inwardly, he hoped the naive woman wouldn't endanger them all by doing something she shouldn't do. He flipped the paper over and wrote out his thoughts on the back, before stashing it with her other writings in the bottom drawer in his desk.

Ginny Interlude

Ginny puzzled over the piece of poetry in her hands and the note on the back written in a masculine hand. She marveled at the courage it took for the newfound family members to leave their home and face uncertain days. She prayed she hadn't made a mistake to take on the project of writing a musical.

Courage sometimes failed her. She navigated her world of classroom and church duties well, but often ducked out of new situations. Taking behind-the-scenes jobs and allowing others to stand in the spotlight came easily. Maybe that was why James found it effortless to claim her work as his own back in college. Well, that needed to be changed. She just hoped she wrote the right thing, something that would make a difference in someone's life.

Jezebel's soulful eyes looked up at Ginny's. The dog pushed in closer and woofed. Ginny grabbed both floppy ears and rubbed them between her hands and the side of the dog's face.

"Thanks for the vote of confidence."

Jezebel leaped away just out of reach and then back, begging her owner to step away from her distractions and play.

"I can do this, Jez, I will write this play. I will chase this dream —and my silly pup."

After playing tag for a few minutes with the hound, she sat down at her computer and started typing. She made herself stay at the desk until her stiff bottom told her it was time to stop.

Missy

Sitting on the carriage seat for several days was taking a toll on Missy's bottom. She wondered if her aunt felt the same way, and yearned to tell George the time had come to find rest for the day. When they'd stopped for a picnic earlier in the day, Early's steps had seemed slower and stiffer. At least one other person suffered. She nudged her sleeping aunt, hoping she'd wake up and feel the same way.

Aunt 'Tilda's eyes squinted open and she stifled a yawn. "Did you need to take a necessary break, Melissa?"

"I thought you'd never ask. I would love to get out for a while and stretch my weary bones."

"You sound like an old woman."

"My body feels like an old woman right now."

"You don't know what you're talking about, child, but it might be a good idea to take a break." Aunt 'Tilda patted her niece's arm and called out for George to stop.

"Yes, ma'am. Looks like there's a house just a ways up the road... It might be a good place to take care of your needs." George rattled the reins and the horses pulled the carriage up a slight rise toward a small white farm house.

As they reached the house, Aunt 'Tilda called out a greeting. A woman stepped onto her small porch and waved to them in welcome as they stepped from the carriage. Missy gazed at the small home and the nearby garden. A lone man rested on his hoe and waved a greeting before picking up a basket of produce and heading their way. She searched for slaves, but saw none. The life she knew focused on homes where slaves did all the work. The only person who seemed at home in this new situation was her aunt. 'Tilda and the woman chattered about vegetables and chickens as they walked toward the small porch. Early and George trailed behind Missy. She wondered if they were bewildered, too.

"Where are your servants?" Missy opened her mouth without thinking.

"We do all our own work here, young lady. The Good Lord gave us two hands to take care of ourselves and that's what we do —wouldn't have it any other way." The woman muttered something about slavery and looked away. "You can make use of the necessary and then be on your way." Her friendly manner fled.

Heat burned Missy's cheeks. "I'm sorry. I didn't mean to offend. We're actually against slavery, too. We're on our way to..."

Aunt's elbow poked into Missy's side and stopped her mid-speech. "Please excuse my niece. She seems to have forgotten her manners. She's going to be working hard to learn about living a much simpler way of life in the very near future."

The woman nodded and led them to the outhouse where they each took a turn. Aunt 'Tilda resumed her conversation with the woman. Before their visit ended, she'd arranged to purchase items for their dinner. The woman grabbed a chicken and stepped to a nearby stump with an axe. The body of the chicken flopped around on the ground after a loud chop. Then their hostess took the beheaded fowl into her house for a few moments before bringing them their chicken.

Missy nearly lost the contents of her stomach when the grinning woman handed her the scalded chicken and showed her how to pull feathers from its dead body. 'Tilda said it would be good practice for being an independent woman. Missy's only thoughts focused on trying to keep her hands clean and unharmed.

She asked Early for assistance, or at the least to find something to plug her nose, but 'Tilda refused to let her cousin help. Instead, her aunt sent Early away with George to collect more vegetables from the farmer's field. Her aunt helped the woman shell peas as Missy pulled limp feathers from the unfortunate bird. Shaking them off her damp fingers and into a bucket filled a good hour of her time. She was glad when the final feather fell into the bucket.

That evening, not far down the road from the farmer's home, they enjoyed roasted meat and vegetables cooked over an outdoor fire. The hard-earned meal filled their hungry stomachs. Missy's tired fingers held a chicken leg up toward the others in a mock salute.

"I hope you are all enjoying my contribution to this feast."

Aunt laughed. George declared it tasted fine.

Early nodded. "I'm glad you learned how to feed yourself today."

A slight stab of guilt and worry filled Missy's conscience as she lowered the chicken to her mouth and savored the meat. She'd completed a small chore today. It would never compare to what Early had done for her throughout both their lives. Would she ever be able to do things without the help of others? Could Early ever forgive her?

That night, despite her concerns, an exhausted Missy fell into a deep sleep. The sounds of crickets chirping interrupted her slumber some time during the night. She and 'Tilda slept on slightly padded benches inside the carriage. She stretched and tried to find a more comfortable position. Peering out a window, she spotted where Early and George slept back to back on the old quilt, under a partly cloudy sky near the waning fire. She missed talking and sharing confidences with her cousin. Clouds covered the moon's shining light as the sound of a few splatters of rain whispered off leaves from a nearby tree. She needed to make things right.

"Early, George! Come out of the rain. We can make room."

Early

A few days later, a man stood in the road and waved them toward his large home. Raindrops misted down on Early's bonnet. The head covering drooped around her face. She had hoped they would stop before it got worse.

"Are y'all looking for a place to stay tonight? I've got some perty nice rooms here at my inn. Your slaves can bed down in the stalls out back. I don't hold to having slaves on my place, but I ain't gonna put 'em out in the rain either." The innkeeper averted his eyes from Early and peered into the carriage window, where Missy sat with her aunt. "The missus has a good bed you two ladies can share. It's clean and what we got's real comfortable."

Early moaned in relief when Aunt 'Tilda gave George permission to head for the inn and barns.

After dropping their satchels on the porch, the innkeeper pointed Missy and 'Tilda toward the inside of the house. He led George and the horse-drawn carriage toward the barn. His personality transformed from hostile to friendly after his wife took the two women into the house. Early trailed along behind the men, listening to them talk about horses and puzzling at the change in mood.

"This little gal's a fine-looking mare." The older man rubbed his hand down the horse's face and pulled a treat from his pocket. She nickered and pushed against his side, begging for more. He laughed and obliged.

"She's a good one. I'm glad the master chose her for our journey." George ran his arm down the side of the animal. Jealousy slithered into Early's heart. Why couldn't he show her some of that affection?

The man freed the mare from the leather that held her to the carriage and led her into a stall full of fresh hay. George stared as the man did his job.

"There's some old quilts in the last stall if you want to make a bed for you and your woman."

Early stomped in that direction. At least she knew how to be useful.

"Are you young'uns happy obeying a master's every whim?"

She turned and looked at George. Would he speak for both of them? He clamped his mouth and gave no clue about his thoughts. Then the older man spoke again.

"It's a little late in the season, but I know a few things about freedom trails, 'iffin you are interested." He raised his eyebrows as he jabbed a piece of straw between his yellowed teeth.

"Really?" George's one word reply brought Early to his side. She grabbed his arm.

"We have to trust Aunt 'Tilda to do right by us."

"She'll do right by you, considering that you're her kin. I know from past experience that not everyone keeps their word to me." George pulled out of her grip and turned toward the man.

"But you are family now—my man. They're taking us nor..." Early gasped and covered her mouth before she let out any secrets.

"Interesting." The innkeeper moved closer. "You think your ladies would take on an extra man for a while?"

"I don't know." Early wondered how she'd had the courage to even consider the possibility.

"It might not be important, but I was in town the other day and saw a message that someone was looking for a slave couple traveling with two women and a perty brown mare."

George's hands fisted at his side as Early edged closer once more.

"If you have someone looking for you, it might change how things look to have two men up top instead of a man and woman." He turned toward Early and studied her face. "Iffin you pulled your bonnet low and covered up good, you could pass for a fine woman inside a carriage with the other gals. Might want to change to a bigger carriage and a couple of sturdy geldings..."

"This mare is like family to me." George finally found his tongue as Early gasped.

"She's liking me perty good right now." The innkeeper scraped a brush across the mare's rump and she leaned into the man. "I see her worth. I'm looking to increase the quality of my herd of horses. I'd trade you a bigger carriage and a pair of strong work horses. You'd have a better chance at freedom and I'd take good care of your little mare, She'd be the queen of my stable."

"The choice isn't up to you two men. The horse belongs to Aunt Matilda." Early turned her back on the two horsemen and trudged toward the quilts in the last stall.

"That's true, little lady, but if I know my missus, she's already been talking to the ladies about your safety. I'm just trying to help by offering you some choices."

Chapter Eleven

Missy

Missy sat on the edge of the lumpy bed and studied the poster the innkeeper's wife had shared. It looked like Sidney was trying to find them. They'd have to make some changes to the way they traveled. Aunt had used up most of her funds to purchase the horse, carriage, and George. Maybe it was time to find a different way of travel, but how could they manage that without extra money? Perhaps they could sell the horse. George seemed sweeter on that mare than he was on his wife. It might serve her best friend well if her new husband had to give up that filly.

A light tap on the bedroom door preceded Aunt 'Tilda's entrance. "Nanny Lee and I have been talking. It wasn't by chance we ended up here for the night. They saw that poster before we arrived and when her Aytch saw us come by their place, he waved us into here for our own protection. There are other inns in the area, but with this one being outside of town, no one else will spot us. It seems they're railway conductors."

"What does the railroad have to do with anything?"

"Oh sweet, sheltered child, they're conductors on the Underground Railroad. They help runaways from slavery find their way north, just like we're doing."

"So, can we catch a train to the north from here?"

"No, child, but we can help with the conducting. It seems they have a man hidden in their hay loft who might be interested in joining our little group."

"Won't we be in danger?"

"No more trouble than what we are already in, since we've become the topic of the poster you're holding in your hand."

"Will our carriage and horse support another person?"

"Unfortunately no, but they've made a generous offer for George's mare and will swap our fancy carriage for an older but larger one and two horses."

"George will be heartbroken over his prize mare. Maybe he'll finally turn to Early for affection."

George

George sat silently as a gray-bearded man climbed up and perched next to him on the old carriage. His mare whinnied from the nearby fence and then nuzzled the pocket of her new owner. Traitor. She wasn't going to miss him much. At least she would be well cared for, perhaps better than he was. The dappled geldings harnessed in the reins he held bore witness to the character of the good innkeeper who made the trade.

The other man and George wore matching gray livery and fancy hats to hide their identities. Earlier, his wife emerged from the inn with the other women. She wore one of Missy's frocks, with her bonnet pulled low over her face. He'd admired her fine figure but hadn't acknowledged her. Too much was at stake. He still struggled with rising anger over parting with the mare. This journey north came with a price.

~~~~~

Hours later, he pushed his hat down firmer on his head as wind gusted through the air. Thunder rumbled in the distance. The team picked up their speed. They'd need to find a barn soon or take the chance of riding out the weather alongside the road. He didn't know the horses well enough to predict how they would handle a storm. Rain began to spatter down. Both horses became more skittish with each boom of thunder. Idle chatter coming from the ladies had grown silent. The quiet man next to him pointed to their right. George caught sight of a barn in the distance as torrents of cold rain poured from his hat and down his back. The horses felt the urgency and quickened their pace. They reached the open doors of the barn and the two men ducked low as the team pulled to a stop. George set the brakes and leaped down.

For once he checked to see how his Early fared before checking on the horses, who huffed with exhaustion and fear. Three wide-eyed women met his searching gaze.

"That was quite a ride!" Aunt Matilda grinned as the two younger women hugged each other.

"Are you all right, Early?" George reached out and took her hand.
~~~~~

She fell into his arms. "We are. Praise the Lord, and thanks to your horse handling we made it." Her body was warm against his. He must be soaking her.

He stepped back. "I'm glad you're all right. I better see to the horses." He stumbled back toward the dripping beasts.

The other man talked calmly to the dapple grays and rubbed their noses down with his hands. "Good hosses. You are sweet boys."

"Thank you for seeing to the horses. I should have asked your name." A deafening boom and flash of light covered the man's answer.

He laughed. "I reckon that was the good Lord giving me permission to change my name. My master called me Job after the sad man in the Bible. I want no more sadness. I want laughter like Sarah had in the good book when she called her baby Isaac. My new name's gonna be Isaac."

"Well, Isaac, I'm pleased to meet you. My mama called me George, so I better keep that name. She named me after an English king."

"Looks like you picked us out quite a castle to wait out this storm in, King George." Thunder still rumbled in the distance as sheets of rain whispered from the roof of the barn. "God sure took care of us today." Isaac rubbed his hand down the quivering shoulder of the horse he attended. George did the same as he pondered the man's words. Had God provided for their safety or were they just lucky to find the barn?

A small hand reached past his to rub the horse's neck. "The new horses did well today."

He draped his arm around Early and drew her closer. He forgot about protecting his heart and allowed feelings to flow over his soul as she snuggled into his side.

"They did. I'm glad we had them. As much as I hate to admit it, they did better than my spirited mare would have done." He wrapped his hand over hers and pulled it across the horse's body. "Follow the direction their hair lays. They will like you better if you go with the nap of their fur." She leaned back against his chest. He closed his arms around her shoulders and rested his head on top of her bonnet. "I like your hair better without the bonnet."

"And I found you quite handsome in your top hat." She twisted around in his embrace and placed a small kiss on his cheek. "Maybe you should teach me more about horses."

"I would love to teach you many things, someday."

He reached up to remove her bonnet just as Missy hissed, "Get back in the carriage, now. It looks like we have company coming."

The rain had turned to a slow drizzle as a spindly man carrying a rifle limped across the field. Aunt Matilda hailed him from the barn door. "Thank you for the use of your barn today. That was quite the storm. I'm sure you welcomed it for your crops."

The man lowered the gun and smiled at the older woman. "Glad to be of help, ma'am. Is it just you and your daughter?"

Missy stepped to her side and nodded a greeting to the man as her aunt replied. "Oh no sir, I'm traveling with two daughters and two men servants. We'll be on our way as soon as we get our horses to back the carriage out."

George and Isaac had their hats firmly in place and began the task of getting out of the barn.

"Where's your other child?"

"Excuse me sir, but she is indisposed with her ah, time of…"

"Never mind." The man stepped away. "Raised three girls myself, so I understand. Those look like fine horses. I was kinda looking for a brown mare. You haven't seen one of those around, have you? I hear they bring top money."

Aunt Matilda laughed. "I wouldn't trade this steady pair for any old mare. Now, we best be on our way before another storm comes blowing through."

George inwardly cringed as he thought of the mare, but bowed his head and silently opened the door for the women. Missy climbed into the carriage and helped her aunt trundle in behind her. Early's bonneted head leaned over as she clasped her belly and quietly moaned. The farmer took one glimpse at her and waved them on their way. As George closed the door, he saw Missy wink at Early. Then the young mistress pulled out her journal and began to write. That woman loved her writing. If they made it all the way north and he got his freedom, maybe one day he would understand her fascination with words. He climbed up on the high bench next to Isaac and started humming a tune. The older man added harmony and tapped a rhythm on his leg as they sang about escaping a paddy roller.

Ginny Interlude

Ginny waited until after the last person exited the sanctuary before climbing up the stairs to sit high on the piano bench next to her friend, Hope. She'd been hesitant to share her songs with anyone. However, she needed to hear how a live rendition of the harmony would sound on her latest compositions. Hope had readily agreed to rehearse the songs with Ginny without knowing they were original to her schoolteacher friend.

Ginny debated about sharing the fact she wrote the song. Doubts concerning her ability to compose made her keep the information unannounced. She didn't want to influence Hope's reaction to the music. The woman's talents lay in art, using cloth from her fabric store as a medium, and also in her resonant alto singing voice. The two women often sang duets for their small urban congregation, so they usually practiced together after services.

"Thanks for staying today. I need to make sure the harmony works for this song."

Her friend's eyebrows rose. "Hmm, Sister, sounds like you might have written this song, if you're checking out the harmony parts. Is it something for our church?"

Ginny felt heat scald her checks, "Uh, no. Annie asked me to write something for the historical museum. I hope I'm worthy of the task."

"Don't you worry, my friend. I've been praying you'd start shining your light a little brighter. This is your chance." She gathered Ginny in a warm embrace and then turned to study the music. "This is really nice. It looks like it might be part of something bigger—want to share?"

"If it all comes together, it will be a musical to raise support for the historical museum. I pray it will possibly make a difference in the whole community. Right now, I'm just forging ahead one song or one scene at a time."

"That's wonderful! Now, let's give this song a run through. It looks like your lyrics may have a message you need to apply to your own life." Hope's voice blended with Ginny's as they sang about a long journey taken by friends to Canaan Land.

Friendship can last when two hearts agree,
To be faithful though they disagree.
The bond of trust may be tried by fire,
But a true friend's love will not fade or tire.

The two women sang through several verses of the song, blending their voices in the sweet harmony of friendship. Ginny penciled in changes where her friend's voice rambled into a better pitch than the one she'd chosen. By the end of their session, though Ginny's back ached from bending over the piano, the song sounded perfect.

Samuel

Samuel tapped the last lead letters into place and pulled the frame tight around the type that would produce the back page of his latest edition of *The Gazette*. His back ached from bending over the tedious task. A little fresh air would be a welcome respite before beginning the next step in the printing process. Stepping across the threshold of the small building that doubled as post office and newspaper office, he arched his back and stared across the street at a group of men.

Bart Simons pointed his way. The other men quieted when they realized Samuel watched them. "Hey there newspaper man, that last paper you printed got a lot of us thinking."

Samuel nodded. "It's always a good idea to do some thinking, neighbor."

Bart sneered. "Yeah, we was thinking that maybe we ought to remind you about the federal law that says you can't be interfering with slave catchers doing their duties."

"I'm aware of the law, but a man's got a right to express his opinion on the matter. That's part of the law of this land, too. Besides, there is a higher authority who might not think much of us having slaves in our land, a land based on the rights of all people."

"That higher authority you're thinking about allowed slavery in the old parts of His book, so don't you go quoting Him to me."

"That's true in a way. Better to say He allowed it and then gave some rules. Slaves were held for seven years and then set free, unless they decided to stay as servants of their own free will."

"Well, we don't want no free blacks roaming around this town, so you ought to be making better choices about what you print in that paper. Last week's poem sure stirred up the bats in some of the ladies' bonnets. They've been harping to their men folk all week."

"Good for the ladies." Samuel nodded and started to turn away.

"Not good for you if this keeps up. Consider yourself warned." Bart and several of the other men heckled with threatening words.

Samuel wheeled back around and crossed his arms. "I must follow my conscience."

A group of women stepped down the middle of the street. They waved to Samuel. Eyelashes fluttered from faces that glanced his way. He felt more fear of the designing women than of the muttering men who began to wander away from Bart's side of the road. Maybe one day soon he would hear again from the young poetess who had drawn him in with her words. A shaft of fear about whether he would be able to resist her sweet charms made him turn tail and close the shop door with a slam. No more women or marriage for him. He had work to do, a press to ink, and pages to print.

The monotonous thump of lifting, pressing, and pulling pages seemed to take forever. His mind wandered. It had been a long time since Aunt Mary Etta or he had received any communication about the travels of Aunt 'Tilda and her entourage. Hopefully their journey through the South brought them few difficulties since they were traveling as slaves and owners. There might be more trouble here in the North once they crossed the Ohio River. It seemed there were many, like Bart and his friends, who didn't welcome those seeking freedom from slavery. He bowed his head and offered a quick prayer for the traveler's safety.

Thump, thump! A heavy rock ripped through the oiled paper covering his front window and rolled across the floor. No message was attached, but the sentiment was clear. Someone did not like what he printed in his paper. He frowned and renewed his efforts to print words for the Cause.

George
Near the Ohio River

The man in front of them frowned. "My best advice would be for you two ladies to travel over on the next ferry with your carriage. I can go along as your driver, as a way of switching up the appearance of your group. You'll be safe enough on that old boat when it crosses the Ohio River. Two women heading north with slaves would draw too much attention."

"But what about the rest of us?" A sense of betrayal washed over George as he clenched his fists. They had almost made it to the northern lands, the free states. The thought that their tickets to freedom would go ahead without them pushed bile into the back of his throat. Isaac stepped away from the group and looked from side to side.

"Don't worry, man. We'll take the rest of ya'll over tonight in another boat, one that won't draw attention. Your lady friends will be waiting at a station house on the other shore. Grab your packs and follow that fellow over there into the woods. He will make sure you find your way."

George shouldered the bag holding enough food to last for a day of separation and grabbed Early's hand. He yanked her forward and heard her yelp in pain. "Sorry," he muttered and slowed his pace as they fell into the last place in line. Isaac walked in front of them, still cautiously looking from side to side. As forest sounds grew silent, the thud of tromping feet grew more noticeable. Someone shushed the group and their steps quieted. Early bent over and pulled a stone from her shoe, then froze. George felt her stiffen and noticed the problem. A bright ray of sun highlighted where a copper and black patterned snake lay curled into itself, probably as scared as the woman whose shoulders he now held.

"Move slowly away, you don't want to startle it or step on it." He put his hands under her arms, lifted her to her feet, and then they inched down the trail. He saw the snake lift its head and slither further into the forest. Tension fell from his shoulders. "You did well, honey. When you have to deal with a deadly snake it is often best to get out of the creature's way. That's what I managed to do most of the time with Sidney. The minute I stepped in his way, he struck back hard and I suffered from his biting whip."

"I'm so sorry," Early whispered as she put her palm on his cheek.

He stepped back and turned toward the trail. They hurried to catch up to the others. He swiveled his gaze from side to side. Hopefully no more human or reptile snakes lay ahead or around them. Darkness soon surrounded the little group. The leader led them to a clearing near the edge of a wide river.

"Look over there at the great Ohio River. Ohio means beautiful in the native tongue. For you, it ought to mean freedom. Just be careful, 'cause some folks don't care what side of the river you're walking on, if you happen to be a black man."

Early clasped George's hand and leaned into his side as a swish-drip sound grew closer to their location. Their leader motioned them toward an approaching boat.

Early

Oars rippled quietly in the water. Dark circles arced out with near silence from the bladed entry points. Their journey brought them nearer to the distant shore. Freedom land lay just ahead. Early felt warmth as George's hand touched hers. She clutched his fingers. Tears welled in her eyes.

"Hey ho, and away we go." Loud voices echoing from the approaching shore shot shafts of fear down her back. The rower paused and signaled with an open hand. They flattened themselves against the bottom of the boat as time slowed to a snail's pace.

The distant shouts gave way to a slurred rendition of a popular tune. Another discordant voice, filled with the devil's brew, belted out a shaky drone. Their voices faded into the distance but still the boatman held his silence. The boat drifted downstream. A cloud slid in front of the sliver moon and the oarsman again dipped into the water. Deeper pulls pushed them back on course as the passengers once again filled their lungs with air. Was there something to fear even on the shore of this free state of Ohio?

The reaction of their boatman showed the reality of that fear — even from a couple of sodden drunks taking a walk on the shore. The quiet lap of water against the banks gave hints that they were growing near to their goal. Early gathered their meager bundle of food and pulled it to her chest. George had fisted his hands and drawn himself into a crouch, indicating he would fight any demons that waited on the shore. Their battle might not be over yet. Isaac tensed beside George.

The oars quieted as an owl hoot sounded from the shore. Early jumped when their rower answered with a hoot of his own. His grinning mouth full of crooked teeth flashed in the dim moonlight as he slid into the water and dragged the boat onto the shore.

"Quiet now. Your journey ain't over yet. Trust only the conductors and don't ask them too many questions. The less you know, the better." The hissed instructions chilled Early more than the water and mud that squished under her feet. The free state of Ohio wasn't the Promised Land after all.

Chapter Twelve

Missy

Missy admired her aunt's skill with the horses. The man who acted as their driver on the ferry ride across the placid waters of the river had left them on their own once the shore was out of sight and they had reached a small inn for the night. He bade them safe travels and handed them a scribbled map that would guide them to the edge of a small town where they would meet up with their fellow travelers. The vista from the top of the carriage gave her an entirely different view from the sheltered one inside. Apple trees, heavy with green and slightly red fruits, lined the road they traveled on. The dappled team shook their heads and seemed to be sniffing the air.

Missy lifted her nose and tried to take in the scent herself. She only smelled the horses that trotted in front of the carriage. "Do you think the farmer would care if we took a few apples for the horses?"

'Tilda laughed. "Not if we take the small ones that have already fallen to the ground. They will be a little tart, but the farmer won't miss them and will probably be glad to bid them good riddance. Are you ready to try your hand at being an apple tree farmer?"

"Only long enough to feed the horses." She sighed. "I hope Early and George still had enough food for today."

"Let's make this quick and put aside a few apples for them in case they're hungry, too." Aunt pulled the horses to a halt, set the brake, and pulled the back of her skirt up through her front waistband. Missy stared. "It will make climbing off this high seat easier. Give it a try."

She followed her aunt's lead and easily climbed down from their perch. She could get used to wearing her dress this way, much easier to maneuver than a full hoop skirt. They filled a small basket with the fruit and fed some to the horses. The animals shook their heads and slobbered their way through several apples.

Missy put her hands on the backside of her waist and looked up to the sky. Picking the fruit had put an ache in her back that she'd never dealt with before. After stretching, she loaded the half-filled basket into the carriage. She tucked a cloth across the top to keep the apples secure and slowly pulled herself back up onto the high seat. It seemed harder to climb a second time. Her cousin Early had mounted the side of the carriage for several weeks now. Surely she could manage half a day of riding the high bench with her aunt.

The un-cushioned seat renewed its torture on her bruised bottom. She willed herself to not squirm or complain. She anxiously studied the map that pointed them closer to the rendezvous point.

"Aunt 'Tilda, I think when we join up again with Early and George, we need to have a plan for an event that separates us."

"I agree." Her aunt slowed the team of horses. "My eyes are a little weak for distances. Does that house have a star on the side of it?"

Missy glanced from the roughly drawn map to the house they neared. "I think we've found the right place. We just have to let them know we are looking for our flock of lost birds."

As they drew nearer a man stepped from the barn. A pronged tool held by his side looked deceptively innocent, but Missy wondered about the pain it could inflict if needed for defense.

"Hello friends, what can I do for you this fine morning?"

Aunt 'Tilda greeted the man with a nod. "We're looking for some missing birds that used to travel with us. We heard they might have flown in your direction sometime this morning." When she said the word *birds* her voice strengthened, giving the man the clue he needed.

"I suppose I won't need my pitchfork for anything but a little hay today. If you ladies would like to drive your horses over to the barn, I'm sure we can take care of all your needs." He reached for a halter on one horse and led them near the shelter. He released the horses and focused on their care while the ladies clambered down from the carriage. "You might find your missing birds in the last stall."

Aunt thanked the man while Missy ran to find Early. The couple lay slumbering on a bed of hay. Missy sank to the ground and grabbed her cousin's hand.

"I'm so glad to see you again."

Early blinked her eyes and looked at their joined hands before answering. "We had a scary trip last night. I thought it would be the end of our journey at one point." The hay rustled next to her as George stretched. He stood and moved to help the farmer feed their horses.

Missy released her cousin's hand and asked about their journey. Then she noticed someone missing. "Did Isaac make it across the river, too?"

"He did. Once we were here, a man came and offered to lead people north. Isaac chose to leave with them. He didn't want to wait when an opportunity to be off at once arose. George talked about it, but..."

"But you wanted to wait for me." A flood of hope filled Missy's heart. She had missed her cousin.

"I did, in spite of you making George marry me."

"I'm sorry, Early, it seemed like a good idea at the time."

"I forgive you." She paused and looked toward her husband. "It may work out eventually. I do have feelings for the man. I just have to wait until he realizes what a good thing he has." She met her cousin's eyes and they laughed before giving each other a hug.

"I don't want to be separated from you again."

"I don't either, but thanks to what happened, my loyalties are now to my husband and freedom. You have to realize that some day we will have to part ways." Early looked away as she pulled bits of hay from her hair.

"I know, but in the meantime we need to make some plans in case we are separated on this part of our journey." Missy rubbed her hands together and looked at the others.

"That's the best idea we've had all morning." Aunt 'Tilda joined them in the stall. George leaned over the wood surrounding the side of the stall and listened as they shared their thoughts.

Aunt 'Tilda started the conversation. "If we get separated, we should plan on heading back to the last place we stopped. The slave catchers would most likely think we would keep heading north."

"Make sure to stay under the cover of trees. We may have to travel at night." George's hand patted his pocket. "We can always look for the north star."

"If we do need to scatter, we should have a code word." Early glanced at Missy.

Missy's mind sparkled, remembering some of the code words they had used as children. "I taught Early some French this year.

We could use the phrase: Run! *Tu connais le plan*."

George nodded, "That's easy to understand, but it might work. I recognize run and plan."

Aunt 'Tilda lowered her voice and leaned in closer to the young women. "The man we crossed the river with said to ask about being a 'friend of a friend' or to mention something about 'birds in the woods' if we needed help from those who want to aid freedom seekers."

She paused and looked toward the front of the barn where their host worked, far enough away to not overhear them. "It's important that you all remember that we will be following a river north of this place for a few days. The river will take us to a canal road. If we stay on that road, it will lead us directly north for many weeks. When the canal turns eastward, we'll be a few days from my sister Mary Etta's place, in a town called Forest Glen. Ask for directions to Woodson House. Someone will be able to direct you if we get separated for any reason. I've been told the house sits on a hill and has a similar design to the mansion at Holly Plantation."

The others nodded in agreement and shook the hay from their clothing. George headed for the horses.

Missy stepped from the stall, followed by her aunt and cousin. "Let's get back on the road."

George

George welcomed being back in control of the team of geldings. He'd always relished the feeling. Even when slavery controlled almost everything in his life, he knew what to do around horses. He understood how to make them do their job. Most importantly, he knew how to do it without abusing or harming their bodies or wills. The rhythm of their hooves pulsing against the ground brought a sense of comfort and rightness. He sat alone on his high bench, feeling good about the horses but missing his companion.

Early chose to continue her ride in the carriage with her cousin since they'd resumed their trek north. The two young women seemed to have renewed their friendship for now. He wondered how long that would last. He wanted to trust the other two women, but still had moments of doubt. At least the last few days of travel had been peaceful.

He scanned the rolling hills of this Free State of Ohio and whistled a made-up tune. When it came to looks, the land wasn't too much different from what they'd traveled through for most of their journey. The soil held a darker hue, but he'd seen that in Maryland as a child. Rolling hills and farmland suitable for growing food for a single family filled the horizon. The rippling sound of water from the river he followed filled his ears with a peaceful sound.

The farmer who housed them after their Ohio River crossing had given him a wide-brimmed hat that flopped low enough to cover most of his face. From a distance, those tending their fields would have a hard time telling his looks from those of any other man. The fellow had managed to find a ragged pair of gloves for his hands. The long-sleeved shirt covering his arms shielded his body from the slightly cooler temperatures.

He wanted to shout 'I'm on my way to freedom' to the world. Instead, he hid under the cover of another man's clothing and kept their carriage moving in a way that didn't bring any unwanted attention. He thought about praying, but decided to leave that up to the women. He hadn't talked to God as much as he should've since those scheming women had forced him into marriage. He had to admit his affections toward Early grew daily. He hated turning his back on her every evening, but it was for the best. They were not free yet. Once they left this peaceful countryside and started traveling along the canal road, they would never know when some other snake might cross their path

Early

Early perched next to George a few days later. The still waters of the canal lay to the left of their path. Open farmland alternated with forested areas spread out to their right and on the other side of the canal. She told George earlier that she'd grown tired of not seeing the outdoors. She didn't want to admit to his face the full truth. She sure missed being next to him as they enjoyed the scenery along the trail.

A sound drew her attention to some tall bushes along the canal road. The red and green leaves rustled among the plants and then human hands parted the branches. Two men stepped from the foliage with guns pointed at the carriage.

"Stop, slave. Get off the carriage or I'll shoot yer woman."

George pulled the horses to a halt. His hand reached protectively in front of her waist. Early felt his body tighten like a coiled snake, ready to spring. One of the men latched onto a horse's halter and stood in front of them, his gun pointed upward to where they sat.

"Looks like we'll be earning a nice bounty for catching you two runaways." Soiled black teeth appeared in the mouth of the dust-covered man who stood to the side of the road. "Get down and move over here, you two slaves." He kept his gun pointed toward Early and glared triumphantly at George as they made their way down.

Matilda stepped from the carriage, hands on her hips. "These are free people. You need to leave them alone."

"Them's your words against mine, old woman." He leered as Missy joined her aunt.

"We have their emancipation papers." Matilda leaned forward, hands on her hips, and then stepped back, holding her nose.

Early gasped. She hadn't realized the papers Aunt Matilda had stashed in her carpet bag contained their freedom, only the proof that they were slaves. She thought for sure they'd have to keep heading for Canaan Land as runaways.

"Give me them papers, lady."

Aunt Matilda glared at the man. "You'll have to find them yourself."

The man reached into the carriage and pulled out several bags. He kicked Missy's satchel of writing materials out the door. It fell open on its side. Pencils flew from the bag along with her journal. Several papers scattered in the dirt, but nothing official-looking fell from the case. Early's worn quilt flew in the air and fell on the dusty path. When he dumped Aunt 'Tilda's carpet bag, he shoved her money into the breast of his shirt.

"Reckon this is part of my reward. Now show me them papers or I'm going to do some shootin'."

The barrel of his gun wavered between Missy and Early. Aunt huffed and pulled papers from a buttoned flap hidden deep inside a pocket of her carpet bag. The man's breath reeked of onions and sour mash as he snatched the papers from her hand and wadded them into a ball.

"Don't reckon these are the real thing, or 'iffen they was, they're gone now. I can't read much fancy writing so it don't really matter none." He tossed the papers into the canal. Ink bled into the water as hopes of freedom sank into murky depths.

"Now we'll see about trussing these two slaves up and be on our way. I reckon this carriage can take us a piece down the road without any trouble." His partner climbed up to the driver's seat and threw down the rope he had looped through his belt.

"You tie 'em up while I check for any treasures up here on top o' this contraption."

The reek of onions once again reached Early's nose as the mouthy man who'd picked up the rope focused on the couple. His mistake. Aunt took that moment to swing her bag across the back of the man's head.

"Run! *Tu connaise le plan.*" As the man swayed, Matilda grabbed his gun and fired it into the air. The sound caused the horses to gallop off with the other bounty hunter bouncing on top of the carriage.

George didn't run. Early watched in fear as her husband growled and knocked the reeling man to the ground. His fists battered the man's face until he moaned and fell into a stupor. Blood and sweat dripped to the ground.

"Stop! Don't bring yourself down to his level. We need to move on." Early found her voice. "You'll be hunted for more reason than just being a slave if you do any more damage to this—this man."

She watched as George unknotted his fists and stepped away. He looked at his bloodied hands and then stared up to the clouds that stalked across the setting sun. He slid down the bank of the canal and pulled out the soaked remains of the papers.

"What now?" His shoulders slumped as paper pulp slid though his fingers and splattered to the ground. Early's heart broke as she stared at the sodden clump that should have guaranteed their freedom.

"First, we need to get away from this man before he wakes up or his partner comes back. Then we can plan our next steps." Matilda grinned and offered the rope to George.

~~~~~
~~~~~

Later that night, they huddled together in the woods. Early sat stiffly next to George on the blanket her mother had created. She listened to the two women, who had been her allies, chatter about possible ways to continue on their journey. Did they even want to acknowledge the feelings of the other two people who sat with them? George grew more distant as the conversation continued.

Early finally blurted out, "When were you going to tell us you had our emancipation papers? I thought you only had owner's papers."

Matilda looked down. "We made a promise to Melissa's father to keep it a secret until we reached Woodson House. We agreed that it might be safer that way."

Betrayal once again flooded Early's heart. First a forced wedding and now this. "It would have been nice to know you had them. Maybe we could have helped protect the papers. We would have known you held the hope of real freedom in your hands."

Missy reached out her hand and then withdrew it when Early crossed her arms. "It's probably too late now, but you should know that at least I have your papers in my possession. We only lost George's today. When Aunt said 'we' had papers, she didn't tell those awful men that we carried them separately. Papa gave me yours as a gift, but he and Amanda's spending habits forced Aunt Matilda to purchase George. The papers gave us ownership, but we changed them to emancipation papers by signing them over to you during a stay at one of the inns along the way."

Early's head swirled with the information. She stepped away from the others. George followed her into a grove of trees and laid a hand on her shoulder. Tears flowed down her cheeks as determination rose from the depths of her soul. The time had come for a change. She turned into George's embrace and laid her head on his chest.

"Do you think we can make it without them?"

"I'm ready when you are. I've always found it hard to trust anyone but myself."

Her throat tightened. "Do you trust me?"

"More than any other person." His palm held her cheek as he leaned closer and brushed his lips across hers.

She returned his kiss with passion. He pulled her closer. They'd not had a kiss this sweet since the wedding. Early's knees felt weak, and she nearly fell when he stepped away. As he drew back, a look of worry crossed his face. He held her by both shoulders and searched her eyes.

"Then we need to make our own plan. We'll follow the drinking gourd stars to the north. I have something that will help us find our way. Are you up for a long walk without a mistress to boss you around?"

"I believe I am." Her voice shook despite her declaration.

"Are you sure? Missy still has your papers. She can safely set you free if you travel with them. Maybe the trip would be too hard for you."

"I'm your wife, George, and there is nothing you can do about that because I made a marriage vow before God. I want to be with you. I want Missy to turn over my papers now." She turned and marched toward her former mistress.

Missy leaned against a tree and rose to meet them as they stepped closer to where she waited alone. Early stopped in front of her former owner and held out her hand.

"I want my papers."

Missy turned away and pulled out the soft leather pouch that hung from her neck and dangled beneath the chemise under her dress. Early had stitched the bag for Missy but hadn't realized what treasure it hid during their journey.

"I'm sorry, Early—sorry for keeping the papers from you and sorry you were forced to be my slave." Sadness etched her face as tears flowed. She opened the bag and slipped familiar pieces of her mother's broken necklace into her palm before offering Early the pouch filled with papers.

Early's tears joined Missy's as she took the bag and stuffed it beneath her own bodice. "I'm sorry you didn't share everything with me. It's time for both of us to grow up and make our own way in this world." Draping her old quilt across her arm, she turned away from Missy and took George's hand before looking around for their other traveling companion. "Where is Aunt Matilda? I should tell her we are leaving."

"She heard a boat coming and went off to see if we could arrange passages since we no longer have the horses and carriage." Missy's shoulders sank as tears rolled down her cheeks. "I only hope she..."

"I have good news." 'Tilda rounded the bend of the tow path and stepped into their circle, looking pleased. "I found a way for at least the women to travel north on a canal boat. We would have to help with cooking and other chores to pay our way. The wife is soon to deliver a babe and will need me to act as her midwife. Maybe George can travel along the canal road until we near Woodson House."

Early faced the other two women. "I will follow my husband. I trust him to find the way north for us. If we happen to see you again at Woodson House, so be it. Otherwise, we will see you in heaven one day." Her voice trembled as Missy and Aunt 'Tilda wrapped their arms around her.

Missy

Missy turned and waved to her childhood companion. They had never been more than a few floors away from each other and neither knew whether they would ever see each other again. Early's mother had raised them both. All she had for memories of her own mother lay in the broken necklace clutched in her hand. She'd lost them all; two mothers, and now her best friend, whom she might never see again.

Picking up her satchel, she placed the jewelry pieces deep inside the bag. She wondered who had the most freedom in the past and the future. Early would know how to take care of her needs — cleaning, cooking, and doing chores. Missy only knew how to be a lady, to paint and write poetry, but how would that help her in a world where no one met her every whim? Could empty words and embroidered samplers put food on the table, if she even had a table of her own? Perhaps she should have stayed and married the McDonald boy. No — not to watch other people like Early suffer at her expense.

She turned to Matilda, "Auntie, you have much to teach me about how to live, how to be strong on my own." Her entry in her battered journal was brief that evening.

Ginny Interlude

Ginny re-read Missy's words of sadness. What would it be like to grow up in a way where she had to depend on another person for her every need? She'd never had that privilege. When her own father had left her mom and his two children, he hadn't looked back. His untimely death did not provide a chance for him to change his ways, so they'd made do. Mom worked hard to provide for the family. Her creativity had provided for their needs and her love had made the three of them feel like a complete family.

Ginny had learned to help with chores as best a child could. Her mother's mom taught her much about life. She and her brother spent many days at Grandma's house while her single parent went to work-related meetings. Those days were long gone. They'd all adjusted to their new way of life. The only lasting effect seemed to be that both siblings tended to be extremely cautious when it came to dating. As she looked at the story unfolding in the journal, she saw a determined spirit in the young woman's writing, despite the sadness expressed on the pages.

The young mistress's life would be very different from living on a plantation, but she would make it. Her mentoring aunt would help her through any trials she faced. The completed journal provided evidence of her survival. While sadness filled Ginny's thoughts for the helpless young mistress, her concerns quickly wandered to Early's journey. Would the two girls ever reunite, or would some greater danger separate them forever?

She wanted to know more about the young couple's travels on the Underground Railroad. Maybe their trek would be what she needed to focus on for the musical, as it progressed. Their way north had to have been full of conflict and drama. She taught her fourth graders to look for those elements in writing their own stories. She'd also taught them about thoroughly researching their topics. She sorted through her pile of books and pulled out a small booklet written in the late 1800s by William Siebert. People kept most of the information about the Underground Railroad a secret. This author revealed some of the major trails that people followed to freedom, years after those avenues were no longer needed. Sure enough, she spotted the canal path marked as a possible trail north in Siebert's manuscript.

A noise at the front door alerted Jezebel, who howled at her top volume.

"Are you hunting someone? You are one noisy hound. I hope

one of your ancestors wasn't a slave catcher's dog." Ginny pushed the hound aside and opened the door for her mother. She wrapped her arms around the woman, wrapped in a festive shawl. "Thank you, Mom, for teaching me how to be an independent woman."

Mom's face showed surprise and then she searched her daughter's face. A few tears dripped from their eyes. "You are welcome, sweetheart. I'm glad you are part of my life, too. Now what brought on this sudden surge of gratitude?"

"I'm just glad you've always been there for me, even when Daddy sailed out of our lives."

Chapter Thirteen

Early

Tears moistened her cheeks as Early lifted her hand. She waved toward the slowly shrinking boat taking Aunt 'Tilda and Missy away. Their figures grew smaller until they disappeared around a bend in the canal.

"Don't start whimpering, girl. We gotta get started on our own journey." George grabbed her hand and pulled her into the tree line. "We have a long night ahead of us. When that's over, we'll find a place to sleep away the day."

"I'd much prefer walking in the day so I can see what I'm stepping on, or into. You know I can't stand snakes."

The enormity of what she had just committed to do threatened to overwhelm her senses. The stench of rancid canal water filled her nose. A large bird screeched as it circled overhead before diving to attack a small blue jay. The slight chill of cooler days ahead blew in the breeze. She crossed her arms and looked in bewilderment at George.

"Day travel will have you stepping back into slavery. From here on out, you won't have Missy to protect you from snakes like Sidney." George stepped farther away from the canal trail. He pulled a round metal object from his pocket. "Look here, Early. I got this compass from an Ohio man who visited during Master Hollings' wedding. It will always point the way to freedom in the north." He popped it open and the needle spun before stopping. "We don't need anyone else." He took a step and motioned for her to follow.

"I thought you said you only needed the drinking gourd stars to take us north."

"There will be nights when those stars don't shine. Then we'll have this compass to show us the way."

She clamped her jaw shut and followed in his footsteps until they found a sheltered place to lay their blanket down for the rest of the daylight hours. Her lips moved in a prayer for safety and a way to control her anger toward Sidney, Papa Hollings, Aunt Matilda, and Missy, who had all betrayed her. Their choices caused her to place her fate into the hands of a husband who seemed more intent on freedom than caring about his wife.

Along the Canal System in Western Ohio

Dearest Mary Etta,

We are sending a separate package your way. It seems that it has become imperative that our goods must make their way north without our help. If they should arrive before we do, please find a safe place for storage, away from prying eyes. Your little den might be the perfect room. The contents are precious to both of us. I do believe they may also be valued by our brother, in his own way.

Melissa and I will be making our way North on the canal system. We finally reached southern Ohio and obtained passage for the two of us on a canal boat. Our journey has endured many mishaps that I dared not share until we crossed the Ohio River. Even then events occurred that altered our plans.

Early in our travels, I had to sell our original horse and buggy in order to continue on our journey. Our driver missed the horse, but he seemed satisfied with the new owners and the condition of their other stock. That change provided one way to avoid attention, which might have been hazardous for our packages. We replaced our horse and carriage for a while, but marauders stole them once we reached Ohio. Most of our possessions are missing too. I'm thankful they threw out Missy's satchel of writing materials when they ransacked our carriage. Otherwise, I wouldn't have paper and pencil for this letter.

Now we find ourselves in a position to work our way north using skills God gifted us with. We will miss our freedom to move on as we please, but are enjoying the company of the canal boat captain's very pregnant wife and independent child. I will be earning my keep as her midwife and cook for a while. Melissa will be learning some important life skills along the way.

Affectionately,

Matilda

~~~~~

Missy

Journal Entry-Somewhere along the canal system in Southern Ohio

A Day of Parting

Today I set my sparrow free.
She'd made a lovely nest for me.
There was no home to call her own,
While weaving me a feathered throne.

Now each must fly to northern lands
To form new homes with our own hands.
She has the talent and the skill.
While all I have are words and will.

If she can fly through briar and bramble,
Find a path where she may ramble,
Then she'll make her nest at last,
In places where no hate is cast.

My flight will take a diff'rent road
I'll learn to carry my own load,
Then one day I'll weave my nest
And gather birds who need a rest.

Those flying north with freedom's zeal
Will need a place to rest and heal.
For now I'll learn new skills for when,
I find a place to settle in.

I pray our flights may cross one day,
I miss my sparrow's soothing way.
But it was right to take our flights
So each of us could have our rights.
~~~~~

Missy picked up her box of Thoreau pencils, replaced the number two in the container and pulled out a number four. The soft pencil provided the perfect tool for sketching and smudging. Early's features formed on the paper as her fingers remembered her cousin's familiar features. They'd been friends forever. Missy already felt alone. The image she drew of her former companion's face would serve as a remembrance of the past and a hope for the future.

Aunt Matilda chattered in the background with the expectant mother and active little girl. They hovered around the small cook stove at the rear of the boat. Their laughter filled the air. Missy sighed and resumed drawing the face, so much like her own, other than the skin color that had held her cousin in slavery. Moments later she switched back to the writing pencil. Aunt had hopes of posting a letter when the boat came to a town. The urge to write a poem for Samuel to use in his paper pulled at her heart. At least she had one useful talent and she thanked God that her poems would help someone realize slavery was wrong. She wondered why slavery existed, as she started scratching out her ideas.

Slavery

Slavery, Why are you here?
Does binding one man to another,
Give you power to make them fear
The master who should be your brother?
You're a dark blight on each heart,
Dividing country, states, and friend.
Piercing hope with poisoned dart.
When will your terror end,
No cage contain my feathered friend?

Early

Early grasped George's elbow and warmth flew up her arm like a bird in flight. His muscles flexed beneath her touch as he lifted a finger to his lips and pulled them further into the woods. The aroma of bacon frying over an open fire filled the air and their bellies grumbled in response. How long would it be before they had another meal? The robbery had left them no choice but to eat what little vegetation George could find in the woods. Had she made a mistake following this man? There'd been no other choice, unless she wanted to return to life as a slave controlled by masters and mistresses. Even Missy had been part of the plans that forced her to marry a man who didn't love her. At least he wanted to protect her.

She pulled her hand away and trudged after him. Maybe she had grown tired of protection. Maybe she should take her own step out on faith. Their hiding from everyone had sure gotten older than the live oaks back on the plantation. Spotting a small branch lying on the ground, she made a decision.

Pushing away from George and the trees that hid them, she plodded down the tow path, leaning heavily on her new walking stick like an old woman. She pulled the quilt over her shoulders like a shawl.

"Come along, old man, we need to keep moving or we will never get to my sister's house before morning."

George pulled his hat down low. He trudged after her, mumbling about stubborn mules. At least he had the sense to follow her lead.

Her imitation of Aunt 'Tilda's accent echoed across the canal waters as she grumbled loudly. "You are the stubborn mule in this family. I should have known better than to marry a horse wrangler that would trade off our last mare for a bottle of whiskey and then drink it all up. Now get a move on, mister, before I use that horse whip of yours on your flea-bitten hide."

George wavered and whooped loudly before stumbling after his wife. A loud burp added credence to the scene they played. Laughter from the campfire echoed as voices cackled about a henpecked husband. If they only knew...

Missy

Splatters of murky water rained down on Missy's seat at the front of the canal boat. No one had warned her that the water-soaked rope attached to the mule team would unleash a rainy downpour on an unsuspecting passenger as they left their first canal lock. The rope had snapped tight when the mules resumed their meander down their pathway beside the water. The submerged rope sopped up plenty of moisture while water in the lock rose to move them to the next level in the system. Missy looked at her damp dress and shook her head. Her only dress—probably ruined, unless she could find a way to clean it herself.

Mischievous eyes locked with hers as a giggle escaped the lips of the captain's daughter. The imp had surely known the water would fall and couldn't contain her full-fledged belly laugh. As a breeze stirred, the dripping water became cool refreshment from the humid air surrounding the boat. Missy chuckled. She needed to thank the Lord for her new acquaintance and the break from the heat.

"Come here, sunshine." She patted the bench and waited for the child to respond.

"My name ain't sunshine." A gap in the child's teeth caused the girl to lisp slightly, adding to her appeal.

"No? Well, you just brightened my day." Missy pulled her sandalwood fan from her waistband and fanned the air, one of the few things the thieves hadn't taken. The child drew closer and settled in to enjoy the scented breeze. The little body added warmth. Missy fanned harder, welcoming the distraction from her thoughts about missing Early.

"My birth name's Elsbeth, but you can call me Sunshine 'iffin you want to." The child squirmed on the hard bench and fingered the embroidery on Missy's sleeve. "Are you a princess?"

"What would make you think that?"

"Your dress is right perty and decorated with this fancy stitching. From what I seen this morning, it don't look like you know how to get dressed by yerself. I saw that other lady helping you get all trussed up this morning."

Embarrassment about being spied upon made Missy's cheeks hotter than any campfire George had built for them along the trail. On the boat, she and her aunt had slept through the night under a light covering, wearing only their chemises and petticoats. Apparently, the child watched them get ready for their day while the captain went on shore to give them some privacy.

"Even I know how to dress myself." The little urchin grinned as she danced off the bench and twirled.

"I guess I used to live like a princess, but that has to change now. Maybe you can teach me a few things about taking care of myself."

"Do you know how to sew?"

"Only fancy flowers and samplers."

"I'll teach you how to do plain sewing 'iffin you teach me about them flowers sewed on your sleeves. Then I can dress like a princess, too."

"You would be a princess for sure and I will appreciate learning how to do some everyday sewing. I don't think I've ever patched a hole in a garment."

"I know all about patchin' rips in clothes. Ma says I'm an accident on feet."

The boat swerved to the right and Missy placed a hand on her stomach.

"You hungry? I can teach you how to fish so you won't go hungry. I'll even teach you how to take guts and scales off a your fish so you can cook it."

Missy grimaced and wrapped her other arm around her belly. "Let's just start with the sewing for now. That should keep us busy for a while."

"First you gotta tell me what it was like being a sort of princess. Did you have lots of servants?"

"I suppose I did, but my favorite servant seemed more like a sister to me. Her name was Early." She reached for her drawing, which thankfully lay protected from the water by the leather satchel. Elsbeth leaned closer to look and touched a finger to the likeness.

"That's a funny name for such a perty lady. Was she always early to everythin'? Ma says I'd be late to meetin' myself if I had to get off our boat to get there."

"She was always there when I needed her. She didn't have a choice." Missy hugged the child closer when her pert little nose scrunched up in a worried expression. "Early's ma took care of both of us when we were your age. She used to tell us that Early came to this world first thing in the morning and that's how she got her name."

"Hey lady, hold on to the rest of your story. How come she didn't have a choice?"

"She lived in slavery."

"My pa says slavery is wrong. Did you do wrong?"

"I did, but I'm trying to change. I set Early free a while back, but someone keeps trying to take her freedom away."

"That ain't right. How you gonna fight for her?" Sunshine punched her fists in the air near her chest, ready to conquer all evil.

"I'm starting by writing poems and stories that are going in a newspaper — and I've been praying some."

"I don't know how writin' can do anythin', but you better do more than just some praying. Maybe I can teach you how to fight and pray better, too."

Missy laughed and picked up her pencil. "I just might write a short poem about my new teacher."

> *A child is my teacher; she'll help me today,*
> *To care for myself, in a most common way.*
> *From stitching to patching, or catching a fish,*
> *We'll learn of a way to meet ev'ry wish.*

"That's a silly one. Can you show me how to make them words that sound alike?"

"I sure can. Rhyming words are a good place to start when you are learning to read and write."

Sunshine leaned over the journal as Missy pointed to the rhyming words and wrote several individual letters for the child. Her young pupil caught on quickly. She took the pencil from her teacher and traced over the words and letters. Then a puzzled expression clouded her sunny disposition.

"Did you teach Early and her ma to read and write?"

"I did, but we kept it a secret from everyone else."

"My ma says not to keep secrets. Did you tell your ma about teaching them about words?"

"No, my real mother died. All I have left of her is a broken necklace." Missy fished the stones from her writing satchel.

"Those are some real nice rocks. I seen some shiny ones like them in a creek one time. Maybe we can figger out a way to sew them back into your ma's neck piece." The child's trusting eyes met Missy's as a barking dog made its presence known from the canal's shore.

George

George ran through the creek and up the muddy bank. His trusting wife followed in his footsteps. Would the dogs find their scent? Had they left the creek too soon? The mud sucked at what remained of their shoes. A chill soaked into the soles of his feet. His restless mind wondered if it was worth the fight. Then he recalled the beating Sidney gave him what seemed ages ago. Better to die in the wilderness than to suffer like that again.

Early's breathing was heavy as he guided her along, but she kept moving. She tripped as she held tightly to his hand, but managed to keep pace. He'd underestimated her strength. She had a good spirit and didn't deserve the future Sidney would have forced on her. He slowed to a stop and listened. The hounds' baying seemed far away. Pulling Early to his chest, they leaned into the dark side of a tree, away from the moonlit sky. She melted into his arms. His Early, his wife, his love, and the mother of his future children, if they could make it to freedom...

He froze when a low voice whispered from behind him, "Follow me."

Did he dare trust the man? He turned and saw a dark figure step away and motion for them to go further into the night. The stranger appeared to be a black man but that didn't guarantee safety. Another man of his race betrayed him back in Virginia. Seeing no other choice, he linked his arm through Early's and cautiously followed the man. Their silent walk seemed to last forever. Their guide led them further away from the canal path they'd hoped to follow. Finally, they paused and saw a group of travelers huddled together.

A woman stepped from the group and pressed a dry biscuit into Early's hand. "Take a bite to strengthen yourselves. We'll be moving on in a few minutes."

Early sank down next to George's feet and pulled him down near her. She ripped the biscuit in half and began chewing on the dry bread. He chose to stay in a squat as he ate. His eyes scanned the rest of the group. Looking up at the sky, he could see the drinking gourd pointing to the northern star. He'd keep an eye on the heavens and make sure the stranger did not lead them astray. The leader took his place and the others fell into a silent line. George and Early followed at the end.

Their weeks became an endless pattern of daytime sleeping followed by night marches through a barely visible path of darkness. Early often sat near the same group of women at dawn each morning. George studied the dark faces in the group and fought the desire to trust the others. Most nights the stars glistened in the sky, leading them north. He could only hope the leader knew the directions when clouds filled murky skies. He wasn't ready to share his precious compass with the others yet.

Chapter Fourteen

Early

Thunder roared. The sky lit from one jagged end to the other. *Boom.* The earth shook.

Their leader urged them forward. "Keep moving folks. This is a perfect night to be making tracks. Ha. Those tracks won't last long in this downpour. Dogs won't catch any scents either."

Torrents of water washed down Early's face as her clothes were plastered to her soaked skin. Could this get any worse? Maybe she was better off being a slave. Too late for thoughts like that now. If someone caught them, her position in the house would be gone. A job in the fields faced her, if she survived the whipping. Her hand reached to the leather pouch hidden under her dress. Would the paperwork make any difference? Probably not, if they sent her back to Holly Plantation...

What had George gotten her into? But she couldn't blame him. She'd chosen to follow her husband and she would stick with him no matter how bad it got. She straightened, but icy stingers ricocheted off her shoulders as she sloshed through a muddy passage made by their leader. The tiny ice balls pinged off hats and tree limbs and plopped against the sodden ground as a chilled breeze whooshed around the group. Her toes froze from the lack of proper covering. She'd replaced the last worn pieces of her shoes by wrapping her feet in rags from remnants of her petticoat. The cloth soaked up the cold water and numbness crept into her feet. She pulled the threadbare quilt around her back with its brown side turned outward. It didn't take long for the rain to soak through.

"Heads down, keep moving." The man was as bossy as any overseer. Early ground her teeth and forced one foot in front of the other. George coughed against the chill and her heart thudded against her chest.

"Are you sick, George?"

"I'll be all right." The gravely sound of his voice said otherwise. Early took the hand that he offered. It was warm—warmer than it should have been on such a cold, wet night. The pounding ice gave way to another soaking rain. Hunger gnawed a pit in her belly. The rumbling sound barely reached ears hearing the gush of rain as it sluiced through the tree branches and leaves. A dark brown form loomed in the distance. Their leader halted them with a warning hand. They huddled on the muddy trail and waited as he faded into the downpour.

George stifled another cough and leaned into her side. Waves of heat poured from his body. A hooded figure stepped near the little group and motioned them toward the dark structure, which took on the form of a barn. The huge hulk of a man threw off his head covering as they entered the hay-filled structure. Whispered instructions sent them up a ladder and into a warm loft. Their host gave each traveler a strip of dried meat, which they quickly devoured. The patter of rain on the tin roof provided a lullaby, sending them each into a warm, but wet sleep.

Early woke several times through the night to the sound of George's raspy cough. She snuggled closer each time, absorbing the warmth emanating from his body, too tired to do more than fall back to sleep as the sun rose and set.

George

The next evening, they left the relative safety of the barn and trudged back onto a trail. The air had grown cooler and chills shook George as they followed the dirt path past a sleeping village. The worn blanket, which had almost dried out during their time in the barn, provided them little relief from the frosty night. A horse neighed in the distance, reminding him of former days when he didn't feel so weak. He should be the strong one, surviving the toils of travel. Instead, his body fought against his will with each step he took. What he wouldn't give for a good horse right now. Grasping Early's hand, he stumbled forward, following her lead like a worn-out nag. Roots seemed to get in his way as their journey continued, bringing him to the ground several times. Colorful leaves cushioned his fall, reminding him of the need to hurry north before even cooler weather arrived.

The quiet leader of their group halted them at the top of a hill and pointed to a small house in a valley. "If any of you are feeling like you need to stop, there's a station house down there. They will take you in for a few days." His eyes looked directly at George.

Early tugged at his arm and asked, "Should we?"

George shook his head. "We need to keep going. I've grown to trust our Moses, but I'm not so sure about anyone else."

Their leader shook his head. "Thank you for your trust, but you better try to control that cough. You don't need to betray the rest of the folks with your noise." He turned and led the group deeper into a forest where they made beds out of leaves for their rest.

Early

Cold seeped through the thin layer of fallen leaves comprising their bed for most of the day. The brightly colored foliage did little to protect Early's side from the hard ground and from air temperatures reminiscent of winter in the South. Many green leaves still clung to the trees around them, providing shelter from any passersby. George's back against hers provided a little warmth. She hoped his temperature had lowered. As if sensing her need for heat, he rolled over and cuddled closer. His arm encircled her waist as he pulled the ratty blanket over both of them. Early tensed and then relaxed into the curve of his body, soaking in warmth from within and without. His soft snore told her that his actions were probably involuntary, but her imagination soared with hope that one day he would make a conscious choice to hold her in his arms.

For now, she found contentment as they snuggled close and tried to sleep. Exhaustion pushed her eyes closed until sounds of the woods startled her back to alertness. A distant howl followed by a closer one brought another chill to her body. Finally, the foggy day drew her mind into a drowsy state where her thoughts tossed about like a ship in a storm. How long could she bear to continue like this? Doubts and fears held her back from deeper sleep. Only the lingering warmth of George's arm kept her from thrashing about. The heat from his arm seemed even warmer than it had before. Determination gave Early the strength to make a decision George would not like.

She sat up and shook him awake. "We need help, George. You are sick and the nights have grown colder."

"But I don't want to be under anyone's control ever again." His cough echoed through the trees as he slowly stood with her help. Several in the group made shushing sounds.

"Do you think we can hide out here with you making all that noise" Early edged closer to whisper in his ear. "Aunt Matilda said there were helpers along the way if we looked for signs. The quilt on the gate of that last farmhouse we passed told me all I needed to know. Our leader even said good people lived there."

His shoulders slumped. "I don't know who to trust. I'm not even sure I have faith in myself to get us to freedom right now."

"Then trust in God. He's provided people willing to help us if you will give them and Him a chance."

George's knees buckled as he fell to the ground. "Help me, Lord."

"Help us both and let these people be part of your plan," Early added as she hoisted him back to his feet.

The temperature radiating from his arm indicated an infection. He needed attention inside a building, not under a tree in the woods. The group gathered round them, and they whispered prayers for their separate travels.

A short time later, Early and George watched as the last of their companions disappeared into the darkness. He leaned against her as they moved cautiously toward the house they'd passed earlier. A lantern with a blue shade sat in the front window, and the quilt she'd seen earlier gleamed in the starlit night where someone had draped it across a fence at the edge of the yard.

Her confidence wavered as she tapped on the door, which squeaked open to reveal a rosy-cheeked woman. Early quietly spoke the words Aunt had told her to use. "We are looking for a friend of a friend."

The woman ushered them into the cottage. "Thou hast found a friend, indeed. We welcome thee to our humble home. Our accommodations are simple and well hidden." The woman motioned them forward as her man lifted a door in the floor, revealing stairs into a cellar below.

George's much too warm hand clasped Early's shoulder as he slowly stepped forward.

Trust. Could she trust her life and George's to these strangers, who spoke words she had only heard in Missy's Bible?

"Thank you, folks." George's rasping voice shook his body as he staggered down the stairs and awkwardly fell onto a nest of straw, covered with an ancient patchwork quilt.

"I'll bring thee some broth before we close the trap door. There be a chamber pot in the corner for your needs." The mistress handed Early a flickering candle sitting in a metal candleholder. The scents of burning wax and the musty cellar filled the air.

The woman returned a few minutes later with two bowls of broth and a pitcher of tea. "Perhaps a sip of willow bark tea will help thy husband with his illness."

"Yes, ma'am. We appreciate your help." Early started to look down but decided to look into the woman's eyes instead. It seemed the right thing to do now that they were on their way to freedom.

"We do this for the Lord. Do you know Him?" The woman's kind expression seemed genuine.

"We do, ma'am." She hoped that held true for George. Surely his recent prayer had been sincere...

"Good. Then take thy rest." The older woman lifted more blankets off a shelf and offered them to Early before making her way up the stairway and closing the trapdoor above them. The scraping sound of something being moved over the trapdoor echoed across the cellar. A sliver of doubt passed through Early, but then she looked at the provisions and decided she had to trust.

Warmth from the soup filled Early's stomach as she alternately fed herself and helped George sip tea or broth.

He squeezed her hand and smiled weakly. "If I don't make it, at least you can lead a life free of Sidney. Promise me you'll keep going."

"Don't talk like that. You just need some rest."

George slumped into a restless sleep. Early woke repeatedly to wipe his forehead with a damp cloth she kept moistened from fresh water in a porcelain wash basin.

For two days they hid and fought the fever until it began to lessen. Early reached for his still warm hand and they both fell into exhausted sleep.

~~~~~

Hours later, Early blinked as the Quaker woman descended the stairs. A blinding shaft of light almost hid the slender child who stumbled after their hostess. The child stared down at her feet until the woman pulled her forward and guided her toward Early.
~~~~~

"There's sickness in these woods. Thy man has what took this child's family to their graves. Might you consider taking her with you to freedom? She can't stay in this cellar forever. A child needs love and light from the outside."

"I don't know." Early's heart broke.

The child trembled while the Quaker led her to a straw pallet on the other side of the room. "Rest here, child." She faced Early, "I can give her love, but I can't promise her a free life. She would wither like a plant in a drought if she stays in this dark cellar. Give it some thought. I won't bother thee again about this until thou art ready to move further north." The quiet woman nodded at both the child and Early before stepping lightly up the stairs and lowering the trap door into place.

Early stared at her sleeping husband. It seemed he had no plans for siring children. She turned her focus on the girl huddled on the pallet. Her eyes no longer faced the floor, but peered at Early. Candlelight reflected the child's sorrowful features. A scar creased the side of her face. A solitary tear trickled down her cheek. Early stepped closer and opened her arms. Sobbing, the child threw her bony little body into the welcoming embrace. A waterfall of tears soaked Early's bodice.

Drawing on courage and determination, she said, "Child, would you like to be mine?" A nodding head provided the child's answer, but it was all Early needed.

George moaned as he rolled over, revealing droplets of sweat pouring from his brow. Praise the Lord, his fever continued to break. He'd soon discover he had a family, whether he liked it or not.

"What's your name?" Early pulled the little one from her chest and held her hands.

"My name is Sheba. Ma said I was her queen." She brushed a hand across her damp face.

"You can be our queen now, Miss Sheba." A warmth filled Early's chest. She would know the joy of raising a child.

"I'm gonna miss my ma."

"I know, sweetheart. There are lots of folks I'm missing too. Maybe we will miss our folks together. Then we can make new friends when we get to Canaan land."

Sheba moved closer to Early. They snuggled together until

sleep overtook them both, as they rested on the child's pallet.

George

George rolled over and searched the darkness for Early. He still felt weak, but he could tell he had fought the worst of the raging battle that had wracked his body. He yearned to feel her warmth next to him. Hopefully he hadn't given her whatever had waged war on his body. The soft whisper of someone slumbering across the room gave him hope that his Early slept nearby. He rolled over and fell into peaceful slumber.

Hours later, George stared at the two females cuddled up together like a couple of satisfied barn kittens. A tiny shaft of light from a crevice in the home's foundation illuminated their faces. Early stretched and pulled the girl closer. Humming an unrecognizable tune, her hand smoothed down mussed hair that must have tickled her nose. His wife had taken in a stray while he slept through his illness. He pushed up to a sitting position and felt his head swirl and then settle. Weakness filled his limbs. How long had he been ill? He didn't know, but his body told him to take his time with any movement.

He took a deep breath, resulting in a weak, but clear, cough. Thank the Lord for survival and for his kindhearted wife. A flood of peace filled him. He hadn't fully acknowledged the Lord in a long time. Too long. *Thank You, Lord, for giving me Early. I don't know what I would do without her now that she is my wife.* Vague memories of her rubbing down his feverish head trotted across his mind. She'd been there for him in his worst of times. Why wasn't she with him now?

"Early?"

"George! You're awake. Are you feeling better?" She pulled her covers over the child and crawled between the two pallets. "Praise be to God!" Her arms wrapped around George's shoulders and nearly knocked him over.

"You're right, Early. God has been watching over us. I've just been too muleheaded to submit to Him."

"I'm so happy for you George. Your prayers can now join mine as our little trio travels on from here."

"Trio?"

"Yes, trio. Over there on that mat is our new daughter. She's mine, at least. If you know what's good for you, you'll claim her as yours, too."

His arms tightened around her and he started to laugh. His old self would have been arguing and fussing, but somehow he knew God had a hand in providing Early with the family she wanted. God provided when George had refused.

"You sure are one sassy little woman, my Early. I reckon I'll have to keep you and your daughter." Early relaxed against him and joined in his laughter. George pulled her closer. "Does our daughter have a name?"

~~~~~

Two days later, George watched Early and Sheba as they sat on the dirt floor, candlelight flickering across their sweet faces.

"This is how you spell your name, S-h-e-b-a." Early leaned over and scratched a series of swirls and lines across the packed ground.

"See those letters, Sheba? That's your name. If you can learn all twenty-six letters, then you can read."

"Won't we get in trouble for knowing how to read, Mama Early?" Sheba laced her fingers in her lap and looked longingly at the scribbles.

"Not where we are going. We will be free to read or write and no one will tell on us." Early smiled at the child and then turned hopeful eyes toward George.

George nodded. "That's right. We are going to the Promised Land. I want to learn to write my name too, so I can spell it by myself when we get there." He wrapped his arms around his girls. At first Sheba stiffened, but then she leaned closer to him.

Early began to scratch something new into the dirt floor. "This is the letter G."

Interlude Ginny

Ginny flipped to near the end of the journal and was surprised to find Missy's notes, relating Early's adventures along the road. She twirled around the room in celebration. Jezebel bounced with her owner until she grew tired and rolled over for a belly rub.

"You make me happy, Jezebel. So does teaching someone how to read and write. I'm so glad Early learned that important skill and
~~~~~

passed it on to her family." She gave the dog one more rub and turned her thoughts back to her project.

Ginny's studies of the pre-Civil War times had revealed that teaching an enslaved person to read could get both the teacher and the student into trouble. That fact twisted like a knife in her heart. Reading opened doors to knowledge and provided an escape from troubles.

She knew the thrill of teaching a child to read and write. Her first assignment had been in a kindergarten classroom. Seeing the proverbial light bulb sparkle to life in a child's mind as they discovered reading skills still sent a burst of exhilaration through her core. Though she taught fourth grade now, she often had the opportunity to offer struggling students some tactics to help improve their reading ability. Her thoughts skittered to her latest pupil.

The poor child had suffered from neglect and had scars from an abusive situation. The youngster had endured her own form of slavery from parents who punished her severely when she couldn't correctly do their difficult adult chores. Ginny's soul filled with delight when the child finished reading a book on her own. The young girl continued to blossom in her classroom, both mentally and physically. Her foster parents made sure she had plenty of support for her educational needs. They also provided healthy nourishment, which her once emaciated body needed.

Ginny turned to her computer and started typing. She finally knew what scene she would use to start her musical. The opening act would feature a little family on the run from slavery. Their journey north would bring them to a climactic escape through Woodson House.

> *We run north to follow our dream,*
> *On a train which runs without steam.*
> *Our conductor follows a star,*
> *As we walk to a land that is far.*
>
> *Canaan land is filling each heart,*
> *With freedom's hope for a new start.*
> *Each footstep brings us closer to home,*
> *Free to go where we wish to roam.*

No more pain from a master's whip,
No more scars when we fail or slip.
Every step we must undergo,
Takes us further from slavery's woe.

We are a family from this day on,
Through darkest night to hints of dawn,
We'll walk together and reach that land,
Where we'll find freedom in our hand.

Chapter Fifteen

George

A week later, George picked up the bundle of food provided by the Quaker family and followed Early and Sheba out into a starlit night. It felt good to breathe fresh air again and he filled his lungs up without having to fight a cough. The drinking gourd sparkled clearly in the moonlit sky as they stepped down a northbound path. This time they followed a conductor known to the Quaker family. He would take them to the next station along the Underground Railroad. Trust flooded George's thoughts as he acknowledged that God could use others to help him on the trek to freedom. Even if they never made their earthly destination, heaven waited.

They trudged through the night to the sound of rustling leaves that covered the ground. The turning leaves, like those that now flittered down, brushing shoulders and then feet, signaled that cooler weather had become part of their trek. Sheba twirled with the leaves as dawn began to break. Her energy overflowed, unlike her newly adopted parents. Their leader waved his hands to quiet the girl and pointed them to a dense grove of trees, indicating by actions that they should take their rest.

His wife sighed as she lowered herself to the ground next to the girl. George fought a lingering urge to cough as he lay back on the leafy ground next to his family. Early's childhood blanket stretched to cover them all as exhaustion laid claim to his body.

Hours later, his eyes sprang open. The musty air was filled with the familiar scent of horse sweat. He missed caring for a horse, but tonight's smell only brought fear. The sound of leaves crushing beneath clomping horseshoes filled his ears. George tightened his fists. They'd come too far to be found. He had fought before on this journey, and he could do it again. The urge to cough warred with the compulsion to protect. His eyes watered in protest. He would not go willingly. He needed to defend his family, his wife and child. *Protect us all, Dear Lord.*

His dread rose and then faded, as silently as the forest surrounding him. The sounds of the single horse and rider grew fainter. No howling hounds followed the horseman. Tension eased out of his body. Early snuggled closer and gently snored, unaware of the danger that had come and gone. He unclenched his jaw. Someone nearby blew out a stream of air and a quiet, "Praise the Lord."

A man snickered and whispered, "That shore was close. Good thing we're all covered in leaves."

George opened his eyes for the first time since he'd heard the horse. Sure enough, a shadowed blanket of red and yellow leaves covered the group. God's hand had provided once again. George laid his arm across Early and filled his mind with prayers of praise. As sleep began to claim his consciousness, he felt a soothing peace flow into his soul and released a hushed, "Amen." Inwardly, he shouted, *hallelujah*.

Missy

"Oowwee! Help me get through this, Dear Lord, Amen!"

The canal boat rang with the cries of a woman giving birth. Missy's work worn hands ached as she labored over laundry, which the woman had deserted when the child had signaled its impending arrival. Her Bible studies told her that Eve's choices made the laboring process painful. Missy had never been around a birthing mother before, and a shadow of guilt fluttered through her mind. Had the pain of her own birth killed the mother she'd never known?

"I wonder if I'm gettin' a brother or a sister this time. I sure hope it lives. Ma's lost a few that didn't make it this far." Sunshine's usually bright demeanor faded to worry as she twisted rinse water from a faded dress.

"I'm praying for your mother and the child." Missy closed her eyes and lifted her petition. Another cry rang from the captain's tiny room at the back of the boat. She hoped Aunt 'Tilda's hands would be able to work a miracle. The moans kept getting closer together.

Water flew into the praying woman's face. Missy gasped as a smile returned to Sunshine's face.

"Sorry, I was shakin' all the water out for ya. At least Ma won't have to worry about the laundry for a while." The youngster laid the dripping garment over the edge of a nearby box of goods the boat transported. Thankfully, the boat no longer transported a large number of passengers like the men who'd departed at the last stop. The master at that lock had loaded them down with crated goods headed for Toledo.

She reached for another dripping article of clothing and flapped it in the air. The blessed sound of silence filled their ears.

A loud *waaaah* shattered the moment of peace. Aunt 'Tilda gave a shout. "It's a healthy boy!" Sunshine and Missy grabbed hands and skipped around the tub of laundry.

"I reckon Pa will be happy to finally get him a boy." They listened to the captain call out to his new mule tender, "Stop the mules." Once they halted, he left his post of guiding the tiller and stepped into the cabin to see his wife and baby.

Missy hugged Sunshine. "I'm sure he was just as happy when you came along."

The mother's laughter echoed from the cabin as Aunt 'Tilda exited and dumped bloody rags into the vat of soapy water.

"How are those arms holding up, niece?"

"I haven't complained so far." She wrinkled her nose as she looked at the red stains spreading across her once clean water. "I'm not so sure I would ever want to be a mother after hearing the captain's wife complaining all day about her pains."

Her aunt waved her into the cabin. "Looks like she's pretty happy now."

Missy stepped into the small space. She reached out a tentative hand and touched the downy hair of the newborn babe.

The mother smiled at her child, hugging the little one tightly to her breast. "He shore is a cute one. I'm thinking he's gonna look a lot like his pa."

The captain let out a whoop, kissed his wife, and returned to steering the boat. Missy followed the man out and returned to her chore. A grin spread wide across the captain's face as he shouted, "We have a boy. Let's get those mules moving, Johnson."

The man he'd temporarily hired to handle the mules shook their reins and the boat resumed its journey along the waterway. The jingle of harnesses and clomp of feet filled the air. Missy wiped her forehead and bent over the tub of laundry once again. That baby sure was cute, but his ma would be tied to him for a long time, between feeding and changing his soiled clothes. Having a baby could wait a long time. Missy decided she liked being her own woman.

The rules and expectations of the plantation felt like ties Missy had finally freed herself from. Her arms were growing stronger from all the work she'd been doing. She enjoyed having control of her life for a change. Earning her own way on this journey and learning how to do everyday chores filled her with pride. She never would have learned how to do all this on the plantation. Early would be proud of her cousin and former mistress. She closed her eyes, avoiding the sight of blood, and scrubbed the soiled fabric. The sight of blood brought her thoughts to Papa's blood-filled handkerchief after one of his coughing bouts. She wondered if he still lived and if he would be proud to know his daughter could take care of herself. Her stepmother might faint at the sight of Missy's work-worn hands.

She stood and dumped the tub of dirty water all by herself. With little effort, she filled it with clean rinse water and renewed her efforts on the bloody material. Little Elsbeth Sunshine left the baby's side and returned to Missy's side to help wring out the laundry.

Amanda Jones De Hart Hollings
Hollings Plantation

Dear Mrs. Mary Etta Woodson,

It is with deep regrets that I am informing you of the passing of my husband and your brother, Arthur Hollings. He bequeathed his property into the capable care of my son and me. His daughter Melissa seems to have left us on a jaunt with her Aunt Matilda. We are unable to locate her or the two slaves they took with them. If they show up at your home, please let Melissa know that Sidney is heartsick. He longs to comfort her so she can join him as wife and mistress of the plantation. He sends his apologies for being over enthusiastic about his feelings for your niece. Since Arthur left his holdings to us, a wedding would be the proper way to provide a home for the young woman.

Please inform her that she must return the slaves they took from us. It would appear that their papers are missing from the household files. I am sure Melissa knows where they are. We've been posting advertisements throughout the southern states trying to locate my dear stepdaughter in order to inform her of the loss of her father. Let us know if you hear of her whereabouts.

Sincerely,
Amanda

Woodson House

Dear Amanda,

Thank you for letting me know about Arthur going on to his heavenly reward. I mourn the passing of my dear brother. I heard he suffered his last few years with a cough. I only wish he hadn't become addicted to his pipe. At least he knew the Lord and I can only assume that he is now resting in the arms of our Savior.

My sister and niece have not found their way to Woodson House, but I will let them know of his passing if they do stop by for a visit. I will retain your letter and a copy of this one so they are witness to my reply. I pray that you will take good care of my childhood home and those who live and work there. Maybe someday you will consider releasing those held in bondage. The slaves of the Bible only served seven years. Releasing your faithful servants or hiring them back as paid workers would be something Arthur might have come to consider one day. The birth of a new era will soon be upon us all.

Sincerely,
Mary Ella Hollings Woodson

Missy

Missy leaned the baby across her shoulder and gently patted the infant's back. A whimper, a burp, a trickle of something wet on her chest, and a warm cascade down her back happened in a quick sequence. The smell of soured milk and urine filled the air as she lifted the child away. The tiny boy grinned and then started to squirm in his wet clothing. His lips pinched together as he let the world know he needed a change.

Sharon, the captain's wife, laughed from her perch at the back of the boat. "I'd help you, but since Johnson moved on to another job, I've got a ship to steer."

"Maybe I should learn how to steer your boat. I don't think I'm cut out to be a nanny or a mother." Missy grabbed a rag and toweled off the front and shoulder of the dress she wore.

Sharon had shared the patched dress with her temporary nanny when they accepted the ride north on the boat. Switching the frock out every few days with the dress she'd worn when they boarded had worked until today. Her own dress from home still dripped from a fresh washing as it lay draped across cargo boxes. Clouds filled the skies. Hopes of it drying out soon were tiny, like the little boy whose volume increased with each clomp of mule hooves.

Sunshine laid a blanket on one of the boxes and took little Noah from Missy's arms. "Looks like you need someone who knows how to take care of you." She cooed to the child and expertly took care of his needs.

Aunt 'Tilda snickered at the scene as she peeled potatoes for the rabbit stew simmering on the boat's iron stove. The captain provided the meat by hunting early this morning. He arose before the others started their day. Watching the skinning and cutting process made Missy want to skip eating their meal, but her growling stomach told her she wouldn't have much choice at dinner time.

Missy stood and moved to the side of the boat. She'd learned a few things on this trip: mending, cooking, and even some basic housekeeping skills. Some appealed to her while others repulsed her. Why did she still feel so useless? Would she ever measure up? Even Sunshine had more ability to take care of the child than she did. Did becoming a self-reliant person come naturally? She went to the bench where she stored her writing supplies and pulled out her journal.

I have learned how to do many everyday chores, but often

doubt my ability to completely rely on myself. Early helped me for most of my life. I'm glad she will have her freedom. Even in that, I am helpless to do any more than pray for her safety. My aunt now helps when she can, or wants to do so. I think she is pushing this little bird out of the nest little by little so that I can be on my own.

Today I failed miserably as a mother's helper. I'm not sure if I will ever want to bear a child after seeing the pain the mother went through and the daily mess the babe makes. He does have a sweet smile though and his presence fills this little family with happiness. Maybe someday I will change my mind, once I am more skilled and settled.

Early hinted that George wanted to wait for children until they were free. I am beginning to see his wisdom. Children need time and love. They don't need the burden of slavery hanging over their parents' heads.

> *Bless the child afloat in this realm.*
> *Bless the hands that guide the helm,*
> *Of boats which bear them cross the waves.*
> *Protect them all both free or slaves.*
>
> *Guide the hands that raise each child,*
> *Make them strong and undefiled.*
> *May parents show they love each life,*
> *And show their care through joy and strife.*

George

Sheba skipped to George's side and took his hand in hers. "I think you're going to be a good daddy for me." Her feet kicked leaves into the air as moonlight streamed through bare trees.

George laughed at her infectious joy. "Why do you think that?" Pride and growing love for the child filled his chest as he looked down at her. The trust he saw in her eyes made him want to cry, something he hadn't done in a long time.

"When you were sick, I prayed if you were going to be a good daddy, then God would let you live."

"Praise the Lord." He looked up at the glittering North Star. "I'm glad He let me live. I never thought being a father would be in

God's plans for me, but I guess I needed you to show me how to take care of a child."

"So now that you know all about being a father, maybe you and Mama Early should get me a sister or a brother."

He swallowed and thought about telling her that he had no plans to fulfill her wish anytime soon. Her face looked so hopeful that he only nodded. "Maybe someday, sweetie. For now, you are all we need. We need some guidance about being parents to you." He turned to see tears dripping down Early's cheeks as she trudged along behind them. Hoping to cheer them all up, he pulled the compass from his pocket.

"Look at this compass, Sheba. It will guide us north to freedom."

"How can a little piece of shiny metal be a guide?"

"It has a spinner that always points north." He held it out for her to see. The pointer bobbled and then settled into place. "This end points north toward that big star, the one you see just off the end of the drinking gourd in the sky."

Early and Sheba both peered at the small compass. Their shoulders pressed into his sides, warming his body and soul as chilly air surrounded them. "This little piece is an amazing guide. I don't know who thought of putting this together. But I do know God is our compass and He brought the three of us together to be a family."

Missy

Missy's legs wobbled as she left her temporary water-based home and walked a few steps on solid ground. She turned and waved to the captain's family. It seemed like she'd been part of their family forever. They'd become close as they taught her more about living a life without relying on a servant. Learning to sew, cook, clean, and take care of the baby helped her develop skills that would last a lifetime. She'd even taken a turn successfully guiding the tiller of the canal-bound vessel.

Sunshine yelled her good-byes from the boat as she jumped from one crate to another. The captain stood near his mules, brushing their coats, and doffed his hat. His wife, Sharon, stood at the tiller, ready to guide the boat down the canal. Her hand waved to the departing women. Their baby slept in a basket not far from his sister's gyrating body.

"Good-bye, friends!" Missy paused and watched the canal boat resume its trip toward Toledo. She moved her satchel from one hand to the other. "I will miss them."

"I will, too." Aunt 'Tilda stepped up the slight incline and headed toward a path running along a rippling creek. In the distance a church bell pealed out a call to worship. "I'm looking forward to seeing the insides of a church again. I doubt we'll make it in time for this week's preaching, but we should be around for the next service." 'Tilda's steps quickened as they walked the path toward a small village.

"I wonder if Early and George made it to Forest Glen ahead of us." Missy's concern grew for her friend as she contemplated walking the whole way they had traveled on the water.

"Their journey will be much longer and tiring than ours. It may take them more weeks than we'd care to think about. We can only pray..." Aunt 'Tilda paused and looked around at the land. "Nice flat land for farming. I'll have to teach you how to grow your own food up here."

Missy looked at the dark earth near their feet. "I'm going to miss seeing red soil. Do you think this black dirt will grow enough to support us?" She plodded along behind her aunt as they resumed their trek. It looked like she had another chore to learn.

"According to Mary Etta, the fields here are very fertile. The growing season is a little shorter, but the abundance in her garden makes up for the lack of familiar ground."

Silence filled the air while they trudged along next to the creek. Missy groaned. Her shoes pinched tighter around her tired feet. "How much longer until we reach Woodson House?"

"My dear niece, I have never been there before. I've only read about it in letters. The creek will lead us into a ravine and Woodson House will sit high on the hill. Mary Etta told me it will resemble your old home, just much smaller in size. Mr. Woodson wanted to make my sister happy by giving her a home she would adore. They were deeply in love when he carried her away to the North."

"I wish someone would come along and carry us the rest of the way."

"Think of your cousin Early. She must walk the whole way here from southern Ohio. Imagine how her feet are feeling right now."

"I'm sorry about complaining. I wonder if Early and George's love will one day sweep them away to happiness." Missy frowned and looked sideways at her aunt. "Did we make a mistake forcing them into marriage?"

Aunt 'Tilda stepped to the side of the path and picked up a stick to steady her steps as they traveled over the rutted ground. "From what I saw when we traveled together, I believe we made the right decision."

Missy nodded and tried to not think about the pain each step caused. Early had always been a strong person, but like her mistress rarely walked long distances. Did she even have any leather left in the shoes she'd worn when they parted? As they hiked along, the flat ground gave way to small rises and then taller hills surrounded the creek.

"Look! I believe we are in the right place." Aunt pointed to a vaguely familiar house that sat straight up the hill above them. All they had to do now was climb the narrow trail that meandered upward. By the time they reached the top, Missy was panting. Even her hearty aunt puffed in her breaths and paused to stretch her back. As they approached the house, Missy noticed a metal W nailed to the chimney that flanked the side of the house. Home at last, or at least home to her Aunt Mary Etta's Woodson House.

The bells from the church pealed again. Worship must be over for the attendees. Missy worshipped in her own heart though, thanking God for His mercies during their travels. The two women sat down on the steps leading to the front porch of Woodson House. Aunt 'Tilda grabbed her hands and prayed a prayer of thanksgiving out loud. Birds chirped around them and a cool breeze blew up from the creek below. A few churchgoers waved curious greetings and stopped to welcome the travelers. It wasn't hard for them to recognize Mary Etta when she rushed to greet them. She looked like an older version of her sister Matilda.

After holding each of them close, Mary Etta held them at arm's length. "Welcome, my weary travelers. I'm so glad that you made it safely." She motioned for them to move up the porch. "I recently got your letter about having to split up from your friends. Do you have any bags that my dear husband needs to carry in?"

Missy held up her writing satchel. "Only one bag. Robbers took everything else. We were lucky — -no, we were more than lucky, the Lord blessed us when we found a canal boat captain who allowed us to work for our ride. We left the captain, his wife, and two children on their boat earlier this morning."

"I'm looking forward to hearing all about your travels. First, let's get you settled inside. I'm sure you are exhausted and hungry."

Missy followed her aunts into the house. The comforts of home surrounded her. Everything was perfect. She only hoped Early and George were nearing the end of their journey.

Samuel

Later that afternoon, Samuel made his way down Main Street and headed toward his aunt and uncle's home. News of the arrival of his Aunt Mary Etta's Southern relatives quickly traveled down the town's gossip line. The information reached his ears as he strolled around town after morning worship. He'd gone home to his lonely table for a cold meal, figuring the ladies needed time to catch up before he blustered his way in to renew an acquaintance with the younger woman. In some ways, he dreaded meeting her again. Maybe her convictions on paper were different from real life. The bubble swirling in his chest told him he feared liking her more than he wanted to acknowledge. Still, good manners dictated that he needed to make a visit to welcome his aunt's relatives to town.

He paused at the door and tapped lightly before letting himself in through the doorway that always welcomed him into his relative's home. "Hello, everyone."

"Welcome, Samuel. I'm sure you remember your cousin, Melissa, and this is my sister, Matilda." Aunt Mary Etta and the other women rose as he neared their chairs.

Samuel bowed to the older woman and held her hand for a moment before he turned to look into Missy's hazel eyes. His breath caught. Her sweet smile pulled at his broken heart strings, strings he had no desire to ever repair. He squashed his reaction by giving the young woman a stiff nod and quick hand clasp.

"I've made good use of your poetry in *The Gazette*."

A puzzled look crossed her face before she settled into her chair and pulled a worn satchel into her lap. "I'm glad you could use my words for the Cause. I wrote more poems as we traveled, if you want to take a look at them." Her hesitant smile spoke only of wanting to use her poetry to help others.

"I would." Good, she wanted to talk business. This he could handle. He took the stack of papers she pulled from her case and leaned back in his chair to read through their lyrical messages. Moments later, he looked up from his reading. "These poems will work well. I see one that will be perfect for the next edition. Do you still want to use a pen name?"

Her eyes seemed to brighten as she declared, "I am not the fearful person I used to be. I would be proud to have my real name published with my poems."

"Good for you, cousin, I will make sure your name appears." Addressing her by the family title eased the discomfort he felt when he first entered the room. Thinking of her as a cousin put a restraint on his emotions and released him to talk business with her. Before long, conversation swung from one person to another as they discussed everything from the weather to the horrors of slavery.

Missy picked up a copy of *The Gazette* that lay on a nearby table. "Samuel, would it be too much trouble to find past copies of the paper with my poems? I'd like to keep them with the journal I wrote during my travels. Maybe one day someone will find my thoughts interesting."

"I'd be glad to get you copies. I usually try to keep several extras each week for my own records. You could stop by the print shop on Monday. I'd be happy to show you the press." He closed his mouth abruptly, realizing he'd offered to have a private meeting with her. That would never do. He glanced at the two aunts looking his way with scheming eyes. "Please bring your aunts with you. I wouldn't want anyone to think we were conducting anything other than business."

"Of course not, cousin, we both know that wouldn't be proper."

He couldn't tell if she mocked him or agreed with his way of thinking.

"We can be friends and workers for the Cause. I have no other expectations. I'm enjoying learning how to take care of myself." She stood and headed toward the kitchen. "Would anyone like me to get them something to drink? I would be glad to serve you."

He gaped as she deftly served everyone cookies and tea. She had definitely changed from the helpless girl he'd met at the wedding reception many months ago. He liked the change, but knew she'd never measure up to his late wife.

As he walked home, he stopped by Rebecca's grave and touched her cold memorial stone. He needed the reminder of what losing a marriage partner did to a person's heart. He would make room for his cousin's friendship, but he would not open his mind to the fact that she bore no blood relation other than through the marriage of his uncle to her aunt. After visiting the cemetery, he continued his restless steps to the edge of the forest. Maybe he'd spot a traveler in need of safety.

Chapter Sixteen

Missy

Several weeks later, Missy pushed away her paper and pen. Her restless fingers ran over the stones in the lavaliere hanging from her neck, which she and Sunshine had pieced together from her mother's broken necklace. That distraction didn't give her any peace. She couldn't sit still. Prowling around the second story room, she peered out the window. Would Early and George make it? Or would some snake of a slave catcher find them and send them south, never to be seen again?

The low grinding sound of her uncle's mill filtered through the open window along with the clomping sound of a horse drawing nearer to the house. The hoofbeats halted and shortly a pounding sounded from the front door. Aunt Mary Etta's muffled voice welcomed someone into the house. Knocking at the front door didn't signal the arrival of her hoped-for cousin and lifelong companion. Her aunt's honey-filled voice echoed up the stairs, telling her of a different caller.

"Melissa, you have company. Samuel has come to call."

A ripple of guilt crossed Missy's thoughts. She had her freedom, but would Early ever really have hers? Even up here there were slave catchers waiting to capture some hapless victim. At least Samuel tried to make a difference. Pasting on the smile she'd been trained to wear on the plantation, she made her way down the stairs and reached for Samuel's welcoming hand. An unexpected thrill made its way to her heart as her smile became real. So unfair that she had hope while Early's life still hung in the balance. Tears formed and trailed down her cheeks.

"Any news?"

"No, but my prayers are with George and Early. Unfortunately, their journey must be much different than yours." Samuel sat across the room in a chair.

"I know, but it seems so unfair." Missy sat on a nearby settee and wondered if Samuel would ever be anything more than a cousin and employer.

"Life is unfair, but God is not. We humans tend to clutter life up with things like slavery and other unjust choices." He reached in his jacket and offered her a handkerchief.

Missy nodded but chose not to answer. She looked toward the window and dabbed the remaining tears from her face.

Samuel cleared his throat. "If they don't come by Christmas, I'll be making another trip down south to let people know there are ways to find their way north. I left a map and compass at the slave quarters on your plantation. Several people seemed interested in coming north if an opportunity opened a door. Maybe someone shared those items with George. I'll also make a stop at Holly Plantation and see if they have been returned." He reached for her hand and briefly rubbed his ink-stained fingers across hers before leaning back in his chair. "Have you written any new poetry this week? There is room for a piece in this week's *Gazette*."

"I've been working on a piece that symbolizes escaping slavery in the south and then facing capture in the north to be like escaping imprisonment in one dragon's castle, only to find themselves hiding in another dragon's den. Do you think people will understand what I'm trying to say?"

"Those who care one way or the other will understand. Just be careful that you don't draw unwanted attention to your other activities."

Late fall near Woodson House

Early

Muddy ground sucked at Early's feet as she and George slowly made their way across the saturated ground. For once she rejoiced that her feet had hardened enough that walking barefoot through the mire actually brought relief. Others in their small group of travelers fought to keep their footwear in place with each step. Their guide called the area The Great Black Swamp of northern Ohio for a good reason. The smell of rotting plant life filled the air with a sour odor that forced several of their companions to pull scarves from their heads and use them to cover their noses. She thanked the Lord for recently closing up her nose with a case of sniffles brought on by the cooler weather.

Sheba's nose worked fine. "I think this smell is going to make me sick." She pulled the front of her neckline up and pinched it across her nose.

George laughed. "I've smelled worse when I cleaned manure from the horse barn."

Their leader stepped near. "Hush, folks, you gotta keep your talking to a whisper. We don't want to be spotted by a slave catcher when we're getting so close to freedom."

George muttered an apology and kept plodding through the slime. The covering over Sheba's face muffled her answer.

Early sloshed closer to their guide and whispered, "Are we getting closer to Forest Glen?"

The man answered in hushed tones, "We should be pretty close by the middle of tonight's travels. Why do you ask?"

"I have a friend who will help us. I'd like to go there."

"That choice might be a mistake. We only go through Forest Glen if a bounty hunter is blocking our way. You'd be better to stay with us and get to freedom sooner." The man stepped away to resume leading the group through the mire.

George leaned in closer to Early. "Maybe we better listen to his advice. He knows this land and the places that would break a horse's leg in this bog."

"I want to visit Missy one more time. I want her to know how strong I've become. I want her to see that we have become a real family."

"You want a lot of things, wife. I only want freedom, and the sooner we get there the better."

Early paused and squished her toes in the mud. Was she being selfish or foolish? She needed time to think. "I'll pray about it until we get close to Forest Glen, but if I still feel like going to see Missy is the right choice, then that's what I hope to do."

George nodded. "I'll be praying, too."

Sheba poked her head between the two. "I'll be praying for whatever gets us out of this muddy devil's hole."

"Keep your mind on God, not that old serpent," Early chided her daughter, and prayed no snakes crossed their path. The chill in the air would work in their favor on that account.

The group moved ahead. For hours the only sound came from

the mud trying to swallow their feet. When the moon reached its highest point above their heads, their guide halted the group and stepped back to Early's family.

"The creek over there will lead you to Forest Glen. You'll cross a canal and then keep following the stream until you get into hill country. You'll see the town sitting at the top of a ravine above this creek."

Sheba tugged on Early's sleeve. "I vote for higher ground."

"I do, too. The description sounds exactly like Aunt 'Tilda described it when she made us memorize how to find the town from the towpath." She took George's hand and squeezed it gently. "I think my prayers have been answered."

"I hope we aren't making a mistake." He shook his head and turned to their guide. "Would you like to go with us?"

"No, we'll be hurrying on our way." The man doffed his hat and once again took his place in the lead. Slurping steps slowly faded into the distance.

Moonlight filtered through the trees. Shadows danced across the well-worn path next to the creek. The sound of water tripping over stones filled their ears as the ground gradually grew firmer under their feet. Their steps slowed when the moon disappeared behind a cloud. A sudden hush of animal sounds made them stop in their tracks and move to the protection of a line of trees and brush near the path. A distant shout echoed across the lowlands, followed by the sound of the firing of a gun. Screams filled the air, followed by muffled men's voices.

Early put a fist to her mouth. Tears trickled down her cheeks. Sheba and George both wrapped their arms around her. For the rest of their night, they huddled together in their hiding place, thanking God for their safety and praying for their recent companions, who once again faced the chains of slavery. When the first light of dawn brightened the sky, they moved further into the woods. George and Early took turns watching over their exhausted daughter and trying to sleep when not on guard duty. The day dragged on. When the sun finally set, she welcomed the night skies that would allow them to travel the next step of their journey.

~~~~~

Early stumbled on a root as they climbed up the ravine in darkness. George's grasp on her elbow kept her from falling. Sheba
~~~~~

trailed behind them like a shadow. The directions given by Aunt Matilda and their recent guide took them from the canal path, along the creek, and then to their steep climb upward. A large house loomed above them. An exposed rock foundation faced the ravine. Shadows of a cellar door faded into the darkness. A dark silhouette of a chimney towered above the house. Would Missy offer help after their strained separation? She hoped so, but their parting had not been on the best of terms. Her breath caught when the door opened and a woman's shadowed form appeared.

The voice that called out quietly spoke in tones she'd been longing to hear, "Are there birds in the woods tonight?"

Missy! She spoke in the code of the Underground Railroad. As her eyes met Early's, the two women rushed to meet each other.

Missy wrapped her arms around Early. Early melted into her friend's embrace until George cleared his throat. Missy backed away and led the little family through a door and into a cellar below the home.

"Who is your young friend?"

"This is our daughter, Sheba. She's been part of our family for a while." Early laughed as Sheba scooted in behind George. "She's not usually this shy."

"If you belong to my friend Early, then you can be my cousin, too. She's always been like a sister to me, but I found out recently that she is really my very own cousin." Missy's cheerful voice filled Early with a sense of belonging and freedom.

"Guess as a true cousin, I can sass you anytime I want." Early gently elbowed her cousin and reached for her hand.

"Yes, friend, you can, and there won't be any consequences other than my sharp tongue." Missy looked at George as he leaned against the rock wall near the cellar door. "I'm sorry we had to leave you and George. You look worn out from your journey."

"It wasn't easy, sister, but I think it all worked together for good, just like it says in the Bible. And maybe the journey gave me courage that I needed to learn how to use." Early stepped back but continued to hold her cousin's hand. "I wish we could stay here with you, but I know we can't. Slave catchers nearly found us yesterday, not far from here. You may be in danger by meeting us tonight. Maybe you should move to Canaan land with us."

"Believe me, I gave leaving with you some thought, but when

I listen to the aunts tell about their work here, I don't think I will. I too have grown stronger. I'm going to help with their efforts to aid people on their way to the North. There's also a group of ladies in this town who are working for the rights of women and freedom for those in slavery."

Missy released Early's hand and wiped a tear from her eye. "I won't ever be going back to the plantation. Aunt Mary Etta received a letter telling of Papa's death and that Sidney and Amanda intend I shall have no inheritance there, unless I agree to marry that awful man. It seems they talked, or tricked, Papa into changing his will. It hurts, but I hold no regrets when there are more important things to be accomplished here."

A loud rhythmic tapping sounded from the floor above them. Missy frowned and put her finger to her lips. She pointed the trio toward an opening near a large fireplace oven. They crawled through and crowded into a tiny room. Early's mouth fell open. The space resembled the hidden plantation room they'd played in as children and where they hid when Sidney tried to find them. The room grew dark as she heard a scraping sound. The room even had a hidden door to seal them in from prying eyes. They'd kept candles in Holly Plantation's hidden room, but based on the commotion coming from above, it would not be a good idea to do anything but sit quietly and pray for safety. She reached for George and Sheba's hands and lifted a silent petition to God. Welcome warmth poured over them. An answer from the Lord, or had Missy started a fire in the oven?

Missy

Missy stepped from the stairway leading to the cellar and loudly announced, "I have the cellar oven started, Aunt Mary Etta. We should stay plenty warm tonight."

The room held more than her aunts, as she'd suspected from the rapped message sent from Mary Etta's rarely used cane. Bart Simons stood glaring at the older women, a copy of *The Gazette* crumpled in his hand. Missy's mind registered surprise that the man would even take time to read the paper because of its abolitionist stand. His reputation as a slave catcher was well-known in the village of Forest Glen.

He tapped the paper against his palm and stepped closer to Missy. "Nice poetry about hiding someone away in a dragon's den. Wondered if you were referring to hiding some runaways here at your aunt's little castle. My friends and I caught a few slaves down in the lowlands the other night. I stopped by to make sure you were safe from any dangerous runaways that mighta come calling."

She swallowed. She'd asked Samuel to use her own name on the last few poems he printed. Bart's sneer widened. She hadn't thought about someone like him seeing the article and actually being able to interpret the hidden meaning. She'd enjoyed hearing how Mary Etta and Matilda had dubbed the plantation's hidden room the Dragon's Den. Having him here searching on the night her cousin and family hid downstairs sent a choking sensation to her throat. She had to clear it twice before she stuck out her chin.

"You need to leave. There is no reason to search our home on the basis of a parable found in a poem."

"If you're harboring slaves, I have every right to look around. If I discover anyone hiding here, you may find your pretty little self sitting in jail tonight." He stood closer and loomed over her. She stepped back and slapped his hand away when he tugged on one of her curls. She'd avoided him in town. Some of her new friends had spoken of his interest in calling on her. Maybe there was more to his search than just looking for slaves. Perhaps it was time to pour on some of the Southern charm she'd used on other would-be suitors.

"So you think I'm pretty?" She fluttered her lashes and settled into a chair with her hand over her chest. "Please be seated and we can reason this out. Perhaps you'd like some tea and cookies."

Bart looked confused for a moment, but he took a seat. His smile didn't quite reach his eyes. "Don't think you can stop me from looking by offering a little sugar. Though, I'm not one to pass up a good dessert." His gaze roved over her body. "I'm still going to do some looking after you try to sweet talk me."

Missy sprang from her chair and hurried to the kitchen. She prayed that Mary Etta still had cookies left in the cupboard. Several ladies had come that afternoon to discuss women's rights and the abolition of slavery. Their children played in the kitchen while the women chatted. She'd left the little ones with her Thoreau pencils, a stack of paper and a plate of cookies. The youngsters were happy for the rare opportunity to use the remnants of her precious pencils, drawing pictures for themselves and notes they left as a thank you for their hostesses.

When she opened the door to the storage room off of the kitchen, she noticed the cozy den-like feel of the little room. The children's thank you drawings sat under a cloth-covered plate near her pencil box. She lifted the cloth covering and revealed enough cookies to offer the slave hunter a temporary distraction. As she picked up the plate, a couple of the drawings caught her eye. She set the cookies back down, plucked a pencil from the box, and made a few adjustments to the drawings. She purposely passed by the bucket of water and nearby tumblers.

Missy carried the plate of cookies from the kitchen and set them in front of Bart. She winced as he grabbed a handful and stuffed them into his mouth. Mary Etta muttered something about teaching him some manners, but he just grinned and scooped the last few crumbs from the plate into his mouth.

Bart swiped his hand across his scruffy face. "Seems like it would have been mannerly to offer some drink alongside these cookies. My mouth has a hankering for something to wash these down with."

Missy bit her lip to keep from smiling too broadly. "Perhaps you should start your search for hidden rooms in the kitchen. We have a bucket of fresh well water in the cupboard room." Her aunts both raised questioning eyebrows in her direction but kept quiet as she barely shook her head.

"I'm guessing you don't have anything stronger than water in this house." He swiped at cookie crumbs stuck to his chin.

"No, we don't. I saw too many drinking problems in my home down south." She placed a hand over her heart and shook her head in mock sorrow as she stepped toward the kitchen.

"I would think a Southern gal wouldn't want to be helping slaves escape." He brushed against her when they entered the kitchen.

"What makes you think I'm helping slaves escape? I know it's against the law. My contribution is found in the words I send to the paper, telling about what I saw as a former Southern slave owner." She laid her hand on his wrist and looked at him as demurely as she could. "Maybe one day you will understand my feelings and we can be special friends." She cringed inwardly as she forced a friendly smile to her lips.

He must have felt her deception. He withdrew from her touch. His eyes searched the kitchen. "Where's that water? My mouth is getting drier by the minute." She pointed him toward the small side room, hoping he would spot the clues she'd left lying around the room. She heard the sloshing of the dipper in the bucket and the swirl of water entering one of the carefully placed tumblers. Peeping around the corner, she watched the paper she'd placed near the tumblers float to the floor. Bart set his glass down with a thump and bent to retrieve the paper.

"What's this supposed to be? Looks like some tot tried to draw a horse with a pointy tail?" He squinted at the drawing trying to make sense of it.

"It looks like a dragon to me." Missy couldn't believe the man had no sense of imagination. "The kids who come here to visit sometimes hide in this room. They call it their dragon's den. If I wanted to hide a slave this would be the perfect place." She looked him in the eye, hoping he would make the connection.

"Humph. I want to believe you, but I'm still gonna look around." He turned and she followed him through the house as he opened closets, checked the attic, and then warmed his hands by the warm oven that heated the cellar room. "Guess you're good for now, but I'm keeping my eye on you, little Missy. You best be careful what you write for that newspaper in the future." He turned and stomped up the stairs. She followed and secured the entrance to the cellar. Mary Etta held the front door wide open as Matilda bid him good riddance.

Early

Early heard the distant thud of a door slamming. Sheba wiggled near her. George squeezed her hand. Had the new danger passed? Nothing stirred above. Not even the quiet taps of a woman's shoes scurried across the boards over their heads.

Sheba whispered, "I don't want to be a slave again."

"You won't. Not while I'm alive." George stretched his arms over Early and Sheba's shoulders.

"Then you both better keep quiet." Early snuggled closer to her husband and grasped her child's hand. The three stayed in their dark room for what seemed like hours before the patter of light footsteps sounded from the basement stairway. A flicker of candlelight shone into Early's eyes as her former mistress opened the hidden doorway.

"You're safe for now, as long as you don't leave this cellar. It doesn't have any windows, so no one can see inside."

"But what if he comes back?" George asked.

"He shouldn't be looking inside again tonight. He might be watching the outside of the house for a while. Once I know he isn't looking, I know a farmer friend who will guide you on your way to another station near Canada." Missy placed the candle on a small table where a plate of apples and bread sat, ready for the weary travelers. She must have brought them down when she came to open the door.

"Thank you, Missy." Early reached for the fruit and handed an apple to each of her family members, before securing one of her own. "You seem to be an active conductor in the Underground Railroad. I'm happy to see my cousin make that choice."

"I'm happy to serve you for a change. You did everything for me in the past. I wish I could have helped more in your journey to this point." Missy looked down and then took one of her cousin's hands. "I'm sure you've had quite an adventure.

"Our travels have been interesting since we parted ways." Early pulled her hand free and reached for the bread. She broke it into pieces for her family.

"I'm glad to see your family has grown."

Early smiled and tugged the unusually timid child forward and hugged her close. "When Sheba's parents went to heavenly Canaan land, we became her parents." She continued her story by telling of George's illness and the kind Quaker woman who introduced their daughter into the family. "We can't share names of anyone who helped us. Most of their names we don't even know. They came from all races and religions, all willing to do what they could to send us toward freedom."

"I wouldn't want anyone to come into danger, but would you mind if I wrote down some of your adventures in my journal? I promise not to use information that would identify anyone."

Early looked to George for confirmation before she made her

decision. His nod and lifted shoulder gave her the assurance she could share what she deemed important. It seemed amazing how they'd grown to understand each other better with each passing day. His eyes spoke of respect, love, and understanding. She smiled back at him before nodding to Missy.

Missy's arms enveloped her with sisterly love. The affection no longer felt like that of a mistress, but as an equal. She returned her cousin's hug as they both cried.

Once their tears faded, Missy retrieved her journal and began to ask questions and take notes. "What do you think your biggest surprise has been so far, on the journey?"

George leaned over Early's shoulder. "I can answer this one. I wanted to do everything on my own. I thought I could make it north with the stars and a compass as my guide."

Missy gasped. "Did you get the compass from a man who came to my father's wedding?"

"I did. The man encouraged us to try coming north."

"My Samuel is the one who gave it to you. He lives here in town."

"Your Samuel?" Early looked at her cousin in amazement.

"Well, not exactly mine. For the present we are both workers for the Cause and that is all. Now George, tell me more about your journey."

Early noted the red that flowed into Missy's cheeks.

"I didn't want help from a white man or woman, but eventually learned that I could trust them, starting with the compass your friend handed me. My biggest surprise happened when I actually saw people who had escaped slavery returning to guide more of us to freedom. I'd heard the rumors of a Moses back in Virginia. I figured she must be something somebody made up, though I placed my hopes in her being real. Then I met with several others along the way who proved me wrong. There are many who act as a Moses to lead their own to freedom." George paused and pulled the compass from his pocket. He offered it to Missy. "Take this to your Samuel and tell him to give it to someone else for a guide. Maybe I can help another by passing it on since we are nearly to Canaan."

As George told the rest of their story, Early's heart swelled with pride. Her George had changed so much. She hoped his love for her had grown, too. They stayed up until nearly dawn, sharing their stories, until Missy could no longer keep her eyes open and their own time for rest neared.

Ginny Interlude

Ginny rubbed her eyes and fought against much needed sleep. No record could be found in the journal, letters, or clippings to indicate how Early's family made their way to Canada. She would have to make an educated guess about the final leg of their journey. She bowed her head and prayed for strength and understanding that would allow her to make her self-imposed deadline for completing the musical. School would be out in another month and if Annie wanted her help with the production, summer vacation would work best for this teacher's schedule.

She needed some quick inspiration, so she pulled her computer keyboard closer. She put in 'Underground Railroad conveyances' and scrolled through the list of sites that appeared. The names of a Quaker couple, Catherine and Levi Coffin, led her to the site of their historical museum.

When a picture of the museum's wagon with a false bottom popped up on her screen, she began to research in earnest. An hour later she had gathered enough information about their wagon to know what type of wagon might have been a likely choice. Forest Glen had several places that boasted of being part of the Underground Railroad. A still standing farmer's barn had hidden runaways in its loft. Rumors surrounding the barn spoke of a possible false-bottomed wagon associated with the man who owned the farm during the pre-Civil War era. Missy's journal had mentioned a farmer who helped her find birds.

Early

Two days later, Missy's farmer friend came before dawn's light broke across darkened skies. He stacked a small load of wood near the back of the house. Mary Etta pretended to direct his efforts and paid him for the wood. The rest of his wagon, loaded with a stack of hay, blocked any view of the cellar door. Early hugged her cousin Missy farewell and crawled into the wagon's hidden space, beneath the hay. George and Sheba slid in on each side of her body. As a closed-in feeling tightened her chest, Early shifted her face to the side and closed her eyes. A short time later, the wagon rocked down the road and she tried to sleep.

A jolt disturbed her restless dozing. The wagon bounced once and then settled into its swaying ride. She had no idea how long they'd traveled. Strands of dry straw and hay tickled her nose. The urge to sneeze felt strong. She pinched her nose closed and prayed no one heard the movement of her arm and hand to stifle a muffled sniff. The walls of the wagon's small compartment pressed Sheba and George's bodies close to hers. A reassuring tap of his fingers against her side sent a quiet sigh of relief throughout her quaking soul. Sheba's soft breathing assured her that at least one family member got some rest.

Breathe. In. Out. Slowly. Silently. The sway of the wagon rocked them gently as it rumbled along. Singing sounded from above their chamber. *Amazing Grace* filled the air outside. As the voice of their driver belted out the words, Early drank in the comforting thoughts. A bump in the road, then silence...

"Morning, Smitty. Looks like a good day."

"Yessir. Perfect day for traveling."

"Where you taking all that hay?"

"Got a brother up in Michigan who got flooded out this year. Thought I'd share some with him and visit a little before cold weather sets in."

"Well, you be careful. I heard some strangers got themselves caught down in the lowlands this week."

George's hand squeezed hers in a tight grip.

"I'm not worried. I got my pistol and whip right here on my lap."

"Well, just keep your eyes open."

Early closed her eyes as the wagon began to sway again. Sheba squirmed on one side while George stiffened on her other. The urge to sneeze again surged through her nose and throat. If she could just hold on a little longer... Her stifled sneeze filtered its way out just as a horse snorted and jingled its traces. "When we've been there ten thousand years" rang out from the driver's seat above her head as George's warm breath tickled her ear.

"That was close, my sweet Early."

She nodded in agreement and thanked the Lord for watching over them.

Chapter Seventeen

George

George pulled his wife nearer and enjoyed having her close to his heart. The cramped space reminded him too much of being confined in crowded quarters with other enslaved people when he'd been shipped away from his family in Virginia. He missed his mama, papa, and the others. He'd always miss them, but Early and Sheba filled up those holes in his soul. One day soon he'd let his wife know how much he really loved her, but not before freedom.

He brushed his lips across her ear and whispered, "Soon..." She snuggled into his side. Her sigh made him whisper, "I love you." He closed his eyes in the already dark space and prayed for safe travels.

Much later, the sways and bumps of their travels slowed to a stop. The wagon leaned to one side and the sound of their driver's feet thumping to the ground changed the focus of George's prayers to a plea that their stop brought hope and not fear. The swish and rocking of someone unloading hay filtered into their hiding place. Another voice greeted their driver. Early shifted away from his side and a chill filled his body and soul. Would this be a safe place? *Father in heaven, keep us safe.*

The hinged wood barrier at the end of their hiding place cracked open. Their driver's face appeared along with his matching image. George thought he saw double for a minute in the light blinding his eyes. Their friendly faces smiled back as they each offered hands to help the trio from their cramped quarters. George steadied himself once his feet hit the ground. He stretched his arms overhead, a gesture of relief and praise to the Lord who had brought them through another step in their journey.

Their driver, still clothed in the homespun shirt and trousers he'd worn this morning, stepped away from his leather-clad twin. "After you stay the night here, my brother will lead you to the edge of Lake Erie. From there, he will get you ferried over to Canada."

Early

As night began to fade into the next morning, Early and her family followed the man down a descending path. Sea birds swirled in the air overhead. Marshy grasses swished against their clothing.

"Are you sure this is the last crossing?"

"I promise, Missus. Once you cross the lake here at Detroit, there won't be any more worries—at least not from them bounty hunters. You'll be in a different country over yonder, Canaan land—better known as Canada."

The fall chill settled onto Early's shoulders as she pulled the ragged blanket around Sheba and herself. The worn quilt made of memories from the past supplied some warmth from the cold. The brown cloth used as its backing had provided a hiding place from pursuers along the trail. George wrapped his arm around both of them as they walked side by side. She had what she needed, protection and love from a husband, warmth from an adoring child. No more running from love, either. Her heart thumped in her chest as her eyes met his warm gaze.

He pulled her closer. "We are almost home, sweet one."

"I hope there's a warm fire when we get there."

"Don't worry, my love. We'll be plenty warm." His whispered implication caused a roll of heat to plunge through her body.

The leather-clad man paused and faced Early. "Don't worry, little lady. You'll get used to the cold after a while. But, for now the society's probably gonna fix you up with a cozy little shack all your own. Come spring, you'll be able to grow a good garden and maybe add a larger crop of children, too."

Garden! So she'd end up in the fields after all. They'd probably starve.

George stiffened. "I've been trained to take care of horses. Is there anywhere I could…"

"Well, what do you know?" The man pulled his fur hat lower on his head as wind whipped across the open waters that lay in front of them. "The commander down at Ft. Malden has been looking for someone to help with his new string of horses." He bent and tugged a boat from the rushes growing along the lakeside. "Seems I heard tell of his wife needing a new domestic the other day... Might take on your woman and girl both... Old Molly's been thinking about moving in with her grandchildren for her last few years. Says her joint pain has been acting up something fierce. I'll let your driver know so he can take you that direction first thing. God must be watching real special when it comes to the two of you, eh?"

"That He is, sir. God has blessed each step we've taken."

Epilogue

Fort Malden
Ontario, Canada

Dear Missy,

So many things have changed since we arrived in Canada. First of all, you can see that I now freely use my reading and writing skills to communicate with you. I am so thankful you took the time to tutor me in all your subjects. I have even found the opportunity to use some of your French words with travelers who pass through Fort Malden.

Late next summer we will be welcoming our own petit bébé into our family. George has his hands full with a barn of well-bred horses and is happy to bring home wages for our table. Sheba and I will continue to work in the commander's house for as long as I am permitted. There is hope that Sheba can continue on once I deliver. After that, I will have my hands full with my paquet de joie. I hope I can remember all the good things Mama shared with us as little ones. My joy will be complete, other than missing you, my sister and cousin. If the wee one happens to be a girl, I will persuade George to give her your name. We have adopted the surname of Freedman and I think Melissa Freedman sounds like the perfect way to start our new lives as free man, woman, daughter, and babe.

Perhaps you can take a sailing excursion across Lake Erie and visit someday. You might be surprised by my accomplishments. Believe it or not, I helped George plant a kitchen garden near our cabin. The seasons are different and so are the crops we can grow in a short period of time. I miss the warm southern breezes, but Canaan land has given me the freedom to love and be loved.

Sending much affection to my sister in all ways,
Early Hollings Freedman

Woodson House

Dearest Cousin Early,

Congratulations on finding the freedom you so deserve. I am excited for the arrival of your petit bébé. I do not envy the travail you will endure when your child arrives. The captain's wife on our canal boat ride gave birth with much discomfort. Fortunately, she seemed to forget her agony when the babe made its way to her arms. You are a strong woman so I know you will be able to quickly forget the process of birth and know the joy of your child. I also hope you can find it in your heart to forget and forgive the past burdens my family placed on you and your George. I am glad to hear you have both found your places in your land of freedom. Knowing you can now be happy in the marriage we forced upon you makes me hope you can forgive Aunt 'Tilda and me for the choices we made.

Thoughts of marriage have crossed my mind from time to time when I am near Samuel. While our fondness for each other has grown, we are both hesitant to move to a deeper relationship, at least for now. The death of his first wife still plagues him, even though it has been several years since her passing. I haven't pushed for him to change. I'm enjoying being a totally independent woman for a change, with no father or stepmother to tell me what to do. Aunt 'Tilda and I are earning our keep by working as typesetters for Samuel's paper. We also print other pamphlets. I'm considering publishing a collection of my poems in the near future.

For now, I am content to earn my wages with ink-stained fingers. Mother Amanda would be appalled and force me to wear white gloves. My newfound abilities fill me with pride in my accomplishments. I think Papa would be proud of me if he still lived. A portion of my wages pays Aunt Mary Etta enough money to cover my room and board. My evenings fill up with meetings about voting rights for women and ways to help other refugees to freedom.

We have to be very careful. Talk of war is growing stronger and people from all over the country argue both sides of slavery and states' rights issues. That may be another reason Samuel is hesitant to mention marriage. He may leave here to fight if a war does erupt.

I hope one day all of this will be a thing of the past and we can freely visit each other again. Maybe by then Samuel and I will have made peace with the past and will be building a future like yours.

Love always from your sisterly cousin,
Missy

Ginny Coda

Ginny hugged the final draft to her chest and closed the door to her home. It had taken the whole school year to write, compose, and edit the musical, but the full manuscript for *Incident at Woodson House* lay in her hands. Annie waited at the museum to celebrate the completed work. The songs and story would tell a fictionalized journey of two cousins finding freedom, one from slavery and one from a life that held others in bondage. It would be a story of love for one and of finding the courage to change for the other young woman.

The story she had framed wouldn't be the exact story from the journals. She'd changed names and circumstances so her main characters both had a happily ever after ending, even though she hadn't experienced that yet in her own life. Her own heart had changed through the year of hard work. Writing the musical had taken away her fear to create. Maybe someday she might also be free to love, as Annie kept hinting. The last song she had written rippled across her heart strings as she strolled toward the museum. Her Song of Freedom...

> *When I reach that final river*
> *And I dwell on Canaan's side.*
> *No more hurting, no more pain,*
> *Once I take that final ride.*
>
> *Freedom's song shall fill my heart,*
> *As I look to God above,*
> *Who brought me cross a troubled sea,*

To a place of hope and love.

No more bondage, no more pain,
No more worries in that land,
Where lost souls, who find their way,
Drop harsh chains and take their stand.

Freedom's song shall fill my heart...

The chorus rang from Ginny's lips and floated on the spring breeze. The song marked the end of one phase in her life and the beginning of another. She praised God for the work. No one knew if the musical would serve the museum successfully as a fundraiser, but its future would be in the hands of extrovert museum curator Annie. Ginny only hoped she could find a few friends to perform her musical on the grounds of the museum. Maybe one of her songs would touch someone's life.

The End

About the Author

Bettie Boswell has always loved to read, compose, and write. That interest helped her create musicals for both church and the schools where she taught. Eventually she decided to write and illustrate stories to share with the world. Her writing interests extend from children to adult and from fiction to non-fiction. *Free to Love* is a prequel to her first novel, *On Cue*. In addition to writing novels, she has written other works including leveled readers, magazine articles, and contributions to lesson plan collections, devotionals, and short story anthologies. She is a minister's wife, church musician, mother of two grown men, and a grandma. She loves the arts and shares her doodles, and photography from her daily walks, on social media.